BAD SWIPE

BILLIONAIRE'S CLUB #12

ELISE FABER

BAD SWIPE
BY ELISE FABER
Newsletter sign-up

This is a work of fiction. Names, places, characters, and events are fictitious in every regard. Any similarities to actual events and persons, living or dead, are purely coincidental. Any trademarks, service marks, product names, or named features are assumed to be the property of their respective owners, and are used only for reference. There is no implied endorsement if any of these terms are used. Except for review purposes, the reproduction of this book in whole or part, electronically or mechanically, constitutes a copyright violation.

BILLIONAIRE'S CLUB

Bad Night Stand

Bad Breakup

Bad Husband

Bad Hookup

Bad Divorce

Bad Fiancé

Bad Boyfriend

Bad Blind Date

Bad Wedding

Bad Engagement

Bad Bridesmaid

Bad Swipe

Bad Girlfriend

BILLIONAIRE'S CLUB CAST OF CHARACTERS

Heroes and Heroines:

Abigail Roberts (Bad Night Stand) — founding member of the Sextant, hates wine, loves crocheting

Jordan O'Keith (Bad Night Stand) — Heather's brother, former owner of RoboTech

Cecilia (CeCe) Thiele (Bad Breakup) — former nanny to Hunter, talented artist

Colin McGregor (Bad Breakup) — Scottish duke, owner of McGregor Enterprises

Heather O'Keith (Bad Husband) — CEO of RoboTech, Jordan's sister

Clay Steele (Bad Husband) — Heather's business rival, CEO of Steele Technologies

Kay (Bad Date) — romance writer, hates to be stood up

Garret Williams (Bad Date) — former rugby player

Rachel Morris (Bad Hookup) — Heather's assistant, superpowers include being ultra-organized

Sebastian (Bas) Scott (Bad Hookup) — Devon Scott's brother, Clay's assistant

Rebecca (Bec) Darden (Bad Divorce) — kickass lawyer, New York roots

Luke Pearson (Bad Divorce) — Southern gentleman, CEO Pearson Energies

Seraphina Delgado (Bad Fiancé) — romantic to the core, looks like a bombshell, but even prettier on the inside

Tate Connor (Bad Fiancé) — tech genius, scared to be burned by love

Lorelai (Bad Text) — drunk texts don't make her happy

Logan Smith (Bad Text) — former military, sometimes drunk texts are for the best

Kelsey Scott (Bad Boyfriend) — Bas and Devon's sister, engineer at RoboTech, brilliant

Tanner Pearson (Bad Boyfriend) — Bas and Devon's childhood friend, photographer

Trix Donovan (Bad Blind Date) — Heather's sister, Jordan's half-sister, nurse who worked in war zones, poverty-stricken areas, and abroad for almost a decade

Jet Hansen (Bad Blind Date) — a doctor Trix worked with

Molly Miller (Bad Wedding) — owner of Molly's, a kickass bakery in San Francisco

Jackson Davis (Bad Wedding) — Molly's ex-fiancé

Kate McLeod (Bad Engagement) — Kelsey's college friend, advertiser extraordinaire, loves purple and Hermione Granger

Jaime Huntingon (Bad Engagement) — vet, does excellent man-bun

Heidi Greene (Bad Bridesmaid) — science, organization, and *Twilight* nerd

Brad Huntington (Bad Bridesmaid) — travel junkie, dreamy hazel eyes, hidden sweet side

Stef McKay (Bad Swipe) — *Stargate SG-1* nerd, her best friend is her golden retriever named Fred

Ben Bradford (Bad Swipe) — closet nerd, businessman, pretends his heart is ice even though it's pure fluff

Additional Characters:

George O'Keith — Jordan's dad
Hunter O'Keith — Jordan's nephew
Bridget McGregor — Colin's mom
Lena McGregor — Colin's sister
Bobby Donovan — Heather's half and Trix's full brother
Frances and Sugar Delgado — Sera's parents
Devon Scott — Kels and Bas's brother
Becca Scott — Kels and Bas's sister in law
Cora Hutchins — Kels' friend since childhood

CHAPTER ONE

Stef

"MARRY ME, FRED," she murmured, tugging her man close and wrapping her arms around him.

He nuzzled into her throat, his warm breath on her skin—

And then started licking her face.

Full stop.

With completely unattractive, smelly breath.

"Ick," she grumbled, burying her face in her pillow to get away from her eighty-five-pound golden retriever.

The only man in her life.

He was hairy, had the aforementioned smelly, doggy breath, but he was loyal and didn't cheat. So, although he would go home with anyone who offered him the smallest morsel of food, his tail always went propellor when he saw her, and he always nuzzled close, especially when she was feeling down.

Yeah, she picked up his shit and waited on him hand and foot.

But how was that different from anyone she'd ever dated?

Spoiler alert . . . it wasn't.

Fred continued licking, thinking her burying herself into her pillows was now the best game ever and attacking her in earnest.

"Okay," she said, pushing him off and sitting up. "Do you want breakfast?"

Breakfast being the magic word, since it sent Fred sprinting from the bed and skidding toward the kitchen, his claws clicking on the tile loudly enough that she could mentally track his path the entire way.

Sighing, she tossed the covers back. She needed to get up anyway, to take Fred on his walk, and then get him off to doggy day care before she headed into work.

Carefully, she shifted out of bed, wincing a bit when she put weight on her ankle.

She'd broken her ankle a few months before—well, Fred and his obsession with a squirrel had been the cause of her injury—and it was still a bit weak and tender. Because of that, she was still going to physical therapy, even though the cast had been off for a while now, and her doc said that she might have to undergo another surgery at some point to remove her "jewelry."

That jewelry being the six screws and two plates currently freeloading their way around town in her body.

And causing her pain when she walked too far or stood too long or, really, just turned in the wrong direction. So truly, it hurt most of the time unless her ass was parked on her plush gray couch or propped up in bed on the special pillow that her friend Heidi had bought for her right after her surgery.

Ah, to be a woman in her thirties.

Sadly single.

Hobbling like a motherfucker.

Pretty soon she'd be bent in half like an old crone, sporting a bedazzled cane. Which—she paused, considered that—might be cool. She could see herself rocking some rainbow sparkles.

They'd go perfectly with her numerous T-shirts and skinny jeans (*and* side part, so take *that*, Gen Z!).

Before she could go too far down her obsession with TikTok, Fred whipped back against the corner, bull in a china shop style.

"Sit!" she ordered, and since he was a good boy, he did just that. Unfortunately because he was eighty-five pounds and had been moving at approximately the speed of light, his sitting didn't mean he actually stopped moving forward.

His ass hit the floor.

His body kept sliding . . . right into the wall.

"Oh, Fred," she murmured as he righted himself just as quickly, sliding some more, his nails clicking on the tile like he was a tapdancing crab until he was finally sitting in front of her.

His tail thumping on the floor.

She stepped by him, careful to not mention the b-word (breakfast), in case he did some more slip and sliding and took her out.

And she did not need *that* on a Monday morning.

"Come on," she said, once she was out of the line of fire, because—like the good boy he was—Fred had waited where she'd told him to sit. And aside from his squirrel obsession, he really *was* a good boy. He was just big and clumsy and all legs and no sense of balance.

Like her.

Ha.

He danced around her legs as she scooped his food, added his vitamins, and then a scoop of supplements that kept his teeth clean and was supposed to battle that doggy breath of his.

Stef wasn't convinced that it helped.

Or it could be a million times worse without it.

Either way, it wasn't something she was going to find out.

Then she sprinkled some shredded chicken because Fred was her boy and yes, he was spoiled as hell.

Once his bowl was in front of him and he was scarfing it down, she got the coffee going, and the moment the bitter, smokey fumes hit her nose, she started feeling less like a Monday Monster and more like an actual human being.

Bagel in the toaster.

Cinnamon cream cheese on the counter.

Plate from the cupboard beside it.

To-go mug open and ready to be filled.

Other mug put in place of the pot and filled with the steaming brew. She took a large sip as her bagel toasted, enough to further chase the Mondays away, and then when it was done, she set about slathering on the cream cheese and doing her level best to replace her blood with the spicy, tangy spread.

It was her absolute favorite.

She bought it by the tub at the local bakery—now bakery chain—Molly's.

And by *the tub*, she meant by the *double* tub, because she always (always!) had a spare container in her fridge.

A girl never knew when she might need a spoonful to chase away the reality of being thirty-five and her longest relationship being with a furry, non-human male who liked to pee on fire hydrants.

Sufficiently caffeinated, she went to pull on a pair of sweats and her tennis shoes then tugged her hair back into a ponytail.

The moment she pulled out the leash, Fred stopped licking his bowl. A walk was the only thing that would convince him to get up because he lived his life alternating between thinking he hadn't gotten every last drop from his dish and worrying that he would never ever eat again.

"Come on, buddy," she said as he trotted over, clipping on his leash and reaching for her oversized hoodie.

They'd do a quick turn around the block and then she'd come back and shower, bundle him into the car for doggy day care, take herself to work, and it would be another glorious Monday.

"Joy of joys," she muttered.

But truthfully, she didn't mind the walk, didn't mind the cool morning air on her face, the quiet of the neighborhood. There weren't many cars on the road at this hour, not with the sun still mostly below the horizon, and it was a peaceful way to start her morning.

Just her and her man.

Smiling when Fred did a little butt wiggle as they moved down the front steps of her condo, she set them on a quick pace as they turned right, looped down through the dew-covered grass in the small park at the end of the street, then back up a block over, before turning onto her street and completing their loop.

His tongue hanging out, Fred sprinted back over to his bowl the moment she opened the door and took off the leash, returning to the business of licking up every last crumb.

Stef flicked the lock and headed into the bathroom to shower.

Was *mid*-shower with shampoo suds dripping down her spine when the doorbell rang.

She ignored it.

Continued washing her hair.

It rang again.

Sighing, since she'd just slathered conditioner on, she kept the water running—yeah, yeah, she knew about the drought, but also, she knew it would take even more water to warm up her shower since her water heater sucked ass—snagged a towel, wrapped it around her head, grabbed her robe, and made her way to the front door . . . just as the bell rang for a third time.

A glance through the peephole made her want to spin around and head right back into the shower.

But she also knew that the knocking wouldn't stop.

Not with Jeremy.

Girding her loins, she unlocked and opened the door. "Yes?" she asked, purposefully blocking the opening so he couldn't just stroll his way into her place. He'd lost that privilege when he'd unceremoniously dumped her months before.

"Where is it?" he snapped, shoving at the door so roughly that she stumbled back a step.

Fred spun around the corner, nails clicking, excitement at seeing a new person—any new person, and especially one who'd occasionally fed him in the past—fueling his barreling. "Wait," she ordered before he could burst out the front door and take her on a sprint through the neighborhood.

He waited, skidding to a stop.

She grabbed the door, pushed the panel back, returning it to its previous position of only being open a crack. "What are you talking about, Jeremy?"

"I'm asking where it is," he growled. "And I'm asking where it is *right now*."

Water was dripping down her spine. The cool air that had felt good on her face earlier now felt like shit because she was wet from the shower and fucking freezing. "What the hell are you talking about?"

A sharp sigh. "You know."

Why had she been forced onto this particular merry-go-round so fucking early on a Monday morning?

Did the universe hate her?

Was the god of evil ex-boyfriends determined to make her life miserable?

"No, Jeremy," she said, grasping at the straws of her calm. "I *don't* know. However, if you'd clue me into what you're looking for, I'm happy to tell you."

Silence.

Narrowed eyes and a clenched jaw. God, once she'd thought he was the handsomest man she'd ever laid eyes on. But now as she was looking at him, she could only see an angry, sad man and wonder how in the hell had she wasted so much time being upset about the breakup.

"Vase. Blue with white flowers."

She frowned, searching her brain, before remembering that she did, in fact, have the vase. It was sitting on top of her bookcase and was actually quite pretty. One of the few things that

Jeremy had bought her that she'd actually liked. But, "You gave me that for our anniversary."

His lips pressed flat. "My mom gave it to me. She's flying in today."

Stef read between the lines. He needed it back or his mom would freak the fuck out, and . . . here her petty streak came out because it was so tempting to refuse, knowing that Jeremy would get an earful from his uber-controlling, feelings-hurt-at-the-drop-of-a-hat mother.

It would be glorious.

But . . . *here* her rational streak came out. If she fought Jeremy over this, he would stay, and he wouldn't give up. He'd browbeat her into giving it back, or at the very least, he would annoy the shit out of her until she was so fed up that she chucked it at him.

And then she'd have glass in her entryway, and she'd be further contributing to the drought because she would have another delay returning to her shower.

Namely having to clean up the glass.

Still, it was tempting . . .

Fred whined.

Reminding her that her pupper would eventually lose all self-control and really burst out the front door, equaling more shower delays.

Lastly, now that she remembered the vase and knew that it hadn't been a gift from Jeremy but rather a regift from his mother, the pretty blue container had lost most of its appeal.

"Wait here," she said.

He narrowed his eyes.

She repeated, more firmly this time, "*Wait* here."

Then she closed the door, threw the lock, and moved to the bookcase. It wasn't far, thus, it didn't take her very long to retrieve it, but Jeremy was already knocking again by the time she made it back to the entryway.

God, why did she have such horrible taste in men?

Sigh.

She flicked open the lock, turned the handle, and thrust the vase at Jeremy. "Anything else?"

He scrambled to hold on to it. "Um . . . no."

"Good." She narrowed her eyes. "If you show up on my porch again, banging on my door, I *will* call the police."

Jeremy's lips parted, anger flooding his blue eyes.

"You remember I have another vase or something else, you text, and I'll get it to you when it's convenient for me." Her voice was harder than it had ever been, and she saw the surprise trailing over his expression. Good. The only positive from this morning's call was that Stef was now certain there wasn't a speck of longing inside her for this man. "Now, go home."

"Stef," he began, and she would have to have been an idiot to not miss the sudden interest in his face.

Nor the way his eyes went to her breasts.

As though the first sign of her temper—which she could truthfully admit wasn't something she'd ever shown him, even in their two years together—was a turn-on.

But seriously, yeah. No.

Maybe she'd been so invested in making the relationship work that she'd hidden parts of herself. Okay, no *maybe* about it. That was the truth. She'd definitely hidden whole facets of herself in order to keep things smooth sailing with Jeremy.

Pathetic. It really was.

Well, no more.

She slammed the door, not caring that it was close to his face, not caring if it *hit* his face.

Then she threw the lock and went back to her shower.

Shutting the door on Jeremy, on the person she'd been with him. Forever.

And good riddance.

For the record, her shower was absolutely divine.

CHAPTER TWO

Ben

HE WAS HALF-DELIRIOUS from jet lag, but he had a full day in the office.

This was the week his company was going public.

And no matter how many times everyone had assured him that all the pieces were in place, shit kept hitting the fan. He was tired of putting out fires. He was tired. Period.

Ben Bradford was thirty-six years old and CEO of a company that was valued at eighteen-and-a-half billion dollars.

He'd never even dreamed something that big was possible.

Not ever.

But it was, and he now had more money than he knew what to do with, money that would grow to an even more ridiculous amount with the IPO.

If only his parents could see him now.

Unfortunately, they were both gone. His dad five years before from a fucking carjacking gone wrong, his mom just the previous year. She'd had cancer, and cancer was a fucking asshole.

So now it was him and his dog—or rather, his mother's dog.

A fluffy Bichon Frise who had typical big-dog-in-a-little-dog's-body-syndrome and whose name was Sweetheart.

She was not sweet, not in any sense of the name.

She barely tolerated him, and that tolerating meant nipping at his heels if he didn't feed her fast enough or take her outside often enough or just happened to walk by at the wrong time and she felt like chasing his ass down the hallway.

But Sweetheart was part of his mom, so he tolerated her.

Plus, she was old, and her teeth were worn down.

Not much damage was doled out, even with the fiercest of heel-nipping.

However, the pet sitter he had on retainer wasn't as convinced, and though she'd been a trooper, he'd received a text the moment his plane had landed telling him that she was sorry, but she could no longer do it.

The evil beast had been fed and watered *and* pottied that morning.

But she needed a break before she could step back into care mode.

A *long* break.

Which meant he needed to retrieve the little asshole that morning and would be working with Sweetheart under his feet —the pooch in a crate that was specially designed to fit beneath his desk.

Just what he needed.

Sighing, he swung by his place, bundled up the pup while ignoring her snarling then jammed her into her carrier because there was no way he was allowing the beast to run free at the office, no matter how dull her teeth were.

Twenty minutes later, he was pulling into his space on campus and moving through the floors with the grumbling, unhappy Sweetheart in tow.

Luckily, he didn't garner any second looks.

Or not any second looks that weren't the usual ones shot toward the big boss walking past offices. The additional second looks that didn't come were those associated with him lugging the pink carrier.

News traveled fast at Hunt Inc., and everyone knew they didn't want to be within fifteen feet of the fluffy white beast who had flunked out of every doggy day care, boarding facility, behaviorist, and trainer, and who'd actually become even worse while on anti-depressants and CBD oil.

Yes, he'd even tried drugging the damned dog.

So, now his life was about his work and trying to mitigate Sweetheart, and no surprise, that was more than enough to keep him very busy.

Maybe once the IPO went through—

Sweetheart went bananas, and he glanced around, trying to figure out what had set her off. Did she see ghosts of doggy boyfriends and enemies past? Was there a person in a thirty-foot radius who'd dared to look at her? Or was she just feeling like her snarling, evil self?

Probably the last.

Likely all three.

Regardless, he managed to get into the elevator, take it up to his floor, and then make the transfer of carrier to crate that finally meant Sweetheart went quiet.

Until he had to take her out to pee.

"For fuck's sake," he muttered, straightening, before moving to the large bank of plate glass windows that looked out onto the city of San Francisco.

In the distance.

Because San Francisco real estate prices were ridiculous.

So, he and Hunt Inc. were situated south of the city, not that the prices were significantly better. This was California. This was Silicon Valley.

It seemed like it cost a million dollars just to own the parking spot his sedan was sitting in five stories below, let alone the entire campus that housed the thousands of employees who worked for him.

But it had all been to get to this point.

His crowning achievement, to be one of the big players, to see his company's name on the stock exchange. A dream, a fantasy . . . and now a reality.

So, why then did he feel so . . . empty?

Nerves because his life was about to change, and it wasn't a small one, because there would be new responsibilities and more people relying on him.

That was it.

The stocks would go live, and he'd feel normal again.

Simple enough.

A knock on his office door heralded his assistants—yes, plural, yes *three* of them—and then Ben was drawn away from the window, from the thoughts of dreams and fantasies and back into the one thing that had always made sense.

Work.

"Mr. Bradford," Baine said, even though Ben had told him hundreds of times before to just call him Ben. "I've got your schedule for the day."

Ben's eyes drifted to Spence who said, "I have those files you requested."

Now Ben's stare moved to Claire, who grimaced. "And *I*, unfortunately, have a problem for you."

No surprise there.

Baine spoke before Ben could. "Meetings are pushed until one. Should give you enough time to deal with this problem and any others that creep up."

Spence set the files on the desk, jumping when Sweetheart snarled.

"Don't worry," Ben told him. "I'm the only one on Sweetheart duty."

Relief flashed across Spence's face. "O-okay. Well, I mean, if you need help with her then—"

"Don't finish that statement," Ben said, stifling a smile. "I know you don't mean it."

Baine, proving once again that Ben hadn't made a mistake in hiring the ex-felon, wove his arm through Spence's and tugged the younger man toward the door. "He doesn't mean it," Baine confirmed, drawing him from the office.

Spence glanced back. "I—"

The door clicked closed.

Claire smiled, shaking her head. "Should I ask about the dog?"

"You already know the answer to that question."

"Right," she said, tapping at the screen of the tablet she carried. "So, I'll just get right down to the newest crisis?"

Ben plunked down into his desk chair, ignoring the rumble beneath his knees.

"Hit me with it."

She did.

And just as all the ones before, it was fucking brutal.

CHAPTER THREE

Stef

FRIDAY EVENING BROUGHT HER FRIENDS, wine, and a throbbing ankle.

At her house for a change.

Oh, and margaritas. Somewhere along the way, Heidi had thought it was a good idea to bust out Stef's rarely used blender, bring up the Drizly app on her phone, and bring in some tequila.

They were celebrating.

Finally, they'd managed to get a clean picture.

Which, Stef got, probably didn't seem like a big deal. But to them—they were molecular physicists, and right now their research was focused on trying to quantify the space between atoms—it was a huge deal.

Difficult because they were trying to quantify something that couldn't be seen with the naked eye, a bit of matter that was surrounded by other bits of matter, including electrons that were whirling around and generally making nuisances of themselves. Flying off in all directions, crashing into each other, joining other atoms and fucking everything up.

But today had gone well.

They'd gotten their photograph, and it was clear, and it was a big freaking deal!

Hence, wine and margaritas, even though at thirty-five, she knew better than to mix her liquors.

The only thing that would make her hangover not horrendous, she knew, was that it was Friday, which meant that tomorrow was Saturday. She didn't do an early morning walk with Fred. Saturday had become beach day, and they did their walk late in the day because she liked to walk the beach at sunset.

The blender whirred, and Stef glanced down at her glass, finding it empty, unsure how that had happened.

Which was fine because Heidi was refilling it, demanding they clink cups and declare, "Cheers!"

"Brad is going to have to pour her out of here," Cora said, her dark brown eyes sparkling with humor . . . and also a bit glazed because she, too, had been partaking in wine *and* margaritas.

"I thought your brothers were in town," Kels said, draining her own glass then holding it up for Heidi to top it off.

"They left this morning," Cora said, slugging back her margarita.

Cora had six brothers, and they'd descended on her small house ten days ago without warning—though probably she should have known they were coming since she'd mentioned to her mom that she'd gone on three dates with a man.

Her brothers were . . . protective.

And that was an understatement.

They were six feet plus, built, and could be scary as shit if they wanted. Not that they used those scary vibes with Cora, Heidi, Kels, Tammy, Kate, and Stef. With women, they were gentle, were sweet and kind and chivalrous.

And single.

Every one of them.

The humanity.

"Fuckers ate me out of house and home," Cora grumbled. "And left me with a mountain of laundry, footprints on the floor, and a new video game system."

Kate's lips twitched, her red hair tumbling over her shoulders. "And that would be any different from the state of your house normally?"

Cora wrinkled her nose. "Shut it, you." Her gaze drifted to Tammy, Heidi's soon-to-be sister-in-law, who had recently moved to town. "Don't keep your childhood friends around. They know too much about you."

Tammy snorted, though she'd wisely just kept to margaritas —although that was mostly because she'd arrived after when the wine had already been consumed.

Kate, on the other hand, gasped and swatted Cora's arm. "Rude!"

"Children," Heidi warned.

"Make another blender full," Kels called. "We're gonna need it."

Heidi set the blender on the counter, picked up her own glass. "Someone else is on blender duty," she said, sinking down on the couch. "I'm done for the evening." She glanced at her watch. "Plus, the boys are going to be here soon, and we all know that Kels—"

"Don't say it," Kels warned.

Cora grinned, stage-whispered, "Is primed for Pound Town when the booze goes down."

They froze.

"Pound Town?" Kels asked. "Seriously?"

Gazes collided. Lips twitched. Then they all broke into peals of laughter—or maybe it was cackling. Either way, all Stef knew was that by the time she gained control of herself, her face ached from smiling, her stomach hurt from laughing, and she was once again so damned happy to have found these women.

They could talk about absolutely everything and absolutely

nothing. They could tease each other until they were sick with laughter, and they would infallibly be there for each other.

No matter what.

Friends. True friends, and not like the ones who'd taken Jeremy's side in the breakup, who'd left her alone in a new state, even though they understood that she'd moved here for him, that her family was back in Florida, and that she knew no one outside of their circle.

Thank God she'd gotten the job with Heidi.

Otherwise she didn't know what she'd have done.

Go back home? Admit that moving to California and quitting her job without a plan, believing in the promise of a man who'd been incapable of fulfilling it, had been a mistake?

Ah. The joy of relationships.

At least her friends had good ones. Heidi's Brad and Kate's Jaime were both amazing. Of course, they were also brothers, so that was probably a big part of it. One family made good men, and it was all the rest of them that—

Tanner was nice, too.

He belonged to Kels.

So, maybe it was that all the good ones were taken?

Or maybe . . . she swore she had a thought there, swirling around her brain, but it flitted away into a fog of alcohol and pleasant sensations as she reclined on her couch listening to her friends babble on about their newest reality show obsession—this one about first dates.

It was sweet and cringy and . . . *just* the thing they loved watching.

"Oh, no," Kate cried, the nicest one of all of them. "He's not going to pick her."

No, the man on the TV didn't appear to be interested in the sweet, nerdy, cute blond girl he'd been paired with. Instead, his eyes were focused over her shoulder, and when the camera kindly cut in that direction, they could all see exactly what had drawn his attention.

A gorgeous, buxom brunette, who was smiling shyly at him.

And yup, now the man actually got up, crossed over to the woman and began chatting her up instead of his own date.

"What a fucking douche canoe," Cora muttered.

"Seriously," Kels said.

"Jeremy did that to me," Stef whispered.

There might as well have been a record scratch for how quiet it went. In an instant, all eyes were on her, and Heidi grabbed the remote, pausing the show. "Excuse me?" she asked, her tone deadly.

"I—um . . ." Stef shook her head. "It's nothing," she said.

"That doesn't sound like nothing," Tammy murmured.

Stef whirled and glared at her. That was *so* not helpful.

Tammy lifted her hands. "Just saying."

"What she's *just saying* is right," Cora said. "Jeremy is an asshole, and you're lucky to be rid of him."

"I am," Stef agreed.

"It's just . . ." Kate began, seemingly plucking the words out of Stef's brain.

Stef winced, decided to not admit to that aloud, and set about glugging down her latest margarita, embracing the burn, grasping tightly to the swirling feeling of her mind.

"It can be hard to start over," Kate continued, thankfully not plucking the second part of Stef's inner thoughts out of her brain.

Because what Stef had been thinking was that it can be hard to be alone.

She shouldn't be feeling lonely.

She had her friends—real, true friends. She had her job. She had Fred, who was currently snoozing in the corner after having exhausted himself and everyone's arms from the copious belly rubs he'd received.

"Yeah," Cora murmured, "it can be."

"Well," Tammy said. "I didn't know the fucker, but if he did that to you on a date, then he was a dumbass. You're beautiful and smart and a total catch."

Stef winced again. "First date."

Heidi's brows rose. Kelsey scowled.

"What a bastard," Kate snapped. She slammed her fist on the table. "The next time I see him, I'm going to take this glass and shove it up his ass!"

There went that fictional record scratch again, the room falling silent for a second time.

Mostly because Kate didn't get mad at anyone, least of all threaten to shove things up other people's derrières, whether or not any of the rest of them thought her target was a worthwhile one.

"One could say I was an idiot for giving him a second date," Stef said. God knew, she'd certainly said it to herself more than enough times.

"Idiot or not, he is more of a douche canoe than the fucker on TV," Cora muttered.

Which earned her a smack from Heidi.

"What?"

"Stef is *not* an idiot," she snapped.

"I—" Stef began.

Heidi held up a finger. "Not one word from you, missy. You are beautiful and kind and smart as shit, and just because Jeremy didn't see that doesn't mean it's any less true."

"Heidi," Stef said.

"It's true and just because the guy had a little dick and—"

"*Heidi*," she repeated, more firmly this time.

"And thinks he's got a pretty face—"

"You've never even met him."

"I saw his picture, and that was enough for me . . ." She trailed off, her glass nearly tipping over in her earnestness to set it on the coffee table. "I knew he was one of those frat boy fuckboys."

"I'm not sure that's actually a thing," Cora pointed out.

"It is," Heidi said.

"Technically, I think it's *two* things," Kels added, both helpfully and not.

"And none of this is really pertinent to this situation," Tammy said, her voice as gentle as her hand patting Stef's knee. "As much as I want to see Kate's attempt at glass shoving."

Stef snorted.

Cora's lips twitched.

Heidi lost it altogether.

Kels merely put a finger up and stated with authority, "The governing board has affirmed Jeremy's status as Douche Canoe and Stef's as Much Better Off Without Him. Now, we shall all drink to that before returning to *First Dates* and—"

There was a knock at the door.

"Curfew," Kate groaned.

But Kels was already tipping back her glass and stumbling to her feet. "My Tanner's here!"

He *was* there.

Along with Brad and Jaime. The three boys having gone to catch a hockey game before returning to gather up the girls. Tanner took Kels and Cora home. Brad and Jaime took Heidi, Kate, and Tammy, since the latter was their younger sister and the newest member of their friend group.

She was wonderful.

They all were.

Even with their drunken shenanigans as they were bundled out the door, trying for one last margarita, insisting on cleaning up, pointing out to their new audience how much of a douche canoe Jeremy was (especially when Kate asked what had happened to the pretty vase that had previously sat on the shelf and had thus been claimed by Jeremy the prior Monday), and then waxing poetic about the wine, the moon, and ironically the pretty pink color of the wax of the candle Stef had burning on the kitchen counter.

Not that Stef herself was immune to drunken shenanigans,

considering exactly what she'd blurted when she was supposed to be watching a silly reality show.

Still, she'd never had anyone stand up for her without reservation, without knowing if she were a hundred percent right. Not before these women.

So, Stef knew she was lucky, damned lucky to have found them.

Even if they had snared the final three good men on the planet.

The damned lucky bitches.

So, she told them.

Which earned her a round of hugs, more cackling, and then, eventually, a quiet apartment.

A quiet, lonely apartment.

CHAPTER FOUR

Ben

SWEETHEART GROWLED at him when he sank down onto one end of his couch.

The end without the tiny set of stairs he'd bought for the damned dog.

So the damned dog could easily get on his expensive couch and make herself at home.

"At home" meant snarling at him if he dared sit down on said expensive couch.

"Shut it," he muttered, sipping on his beer and reaching for the remote. "And I'm not turning on *Dr. Pol*," he added. "No matter how much you like to watch the male animals get castrated, you ball buster." A snort. "Literally."

Smirking at his own joke and ignoring her huff, he kept drinking and turned on the TV, cued up the guide.

His company was public.

The stock price was good, although it was too early to truly tell if his gamble would pay off. Okay, that was a cop-out. He knew it was going to pay off. The company's valuation was solid, investors were pumped, his business was steady and increasing and *steady*.

A good bet.

A great investment.

So, all would be good.

And for the first time in six fucking years, he could take a breath. He could relax. He could . . . do something that would be relaxing. He just needed to figure out what that would be.

Sex.

Yeah, he could do that. He *should* do that.

When was the last time he'd had an orgasm? Okay, and adding to that, when was the last time he'd had an orgasm that wasn't courtesy of his own hand? Months? Years?

Sweetheart huffed again.

He squinted at the guide on the TV, hit something at random, and if that something was *Dr. Pol* then it wasn't because of the ornery dog next to him.

———

BEN JERKED UP, his beer sloshing over his hand, splashing onto his expensive couch, probably staining it irrevocably.

The marathon of *Dr. Pol* was still going strong, a line of empty beer bottles on his coffee table, and—his eyes flicked down—the devil dog was curled up next to his thigh. Sweetheart had her head on his thigh, and when he glanced down at her tiny white head, her lips tightened.

"Shut it," he muttered, lifting the bottle to his mouth then wincing and reaching forward to plunk it on the table, ignoring the displeased sound that she made.

It was nearly midnight on a Friday, and he was on the couch with his dead mother's dog—*drunk* on the couch with the dog because he was so out of practice relaxing that five . . . he squinted . . . *six?* . . . beers meant that he was gone.

Room spinning.

Veterinarian on the TV screen shuffling around.

Dog who was the worst dog in the history of all dogs on his lap.

Months since his last orgasm. Years since his last pussy.

For all intents and purposes, he should be out celebrating with a model on each arm. That was what all the tech guys who made it big in Silicon Valley did. They lived large and partied hard, somehow managing to shed their nerdy roots and revel in the excess.

Well, he wasn't much of an excess guy.

And frankly, he was a nerd all the way down to the marrow of his bones.

Before Sweetheart had highjacked his viewing habits, he'd been an all Sci-Fi all the time guy. *Stargate, Farscape, The Expanse, Van Helsing,* old movies he'd seen a million times. The more out there, the better.

He liked to escape.

His reality had been more than e-fucking-nough.

But the last few years, he hadn't needed to escape—or at least, he hadn't needed *that* escape. Work had been enough. There hadn't been a necessity for fantasy.

Now . . . he was a CEO with some time on his hands.

His phone buzzed, and he reached into his pocket to extract it—much to Sweetheart's displeasure—and saw a notification on his screen.

For an app he'd never downloaded.

You've got a new match.

Trailed by some fucking emojis.

"What the hell?" he whispered.

And then he *knew.*

His fingers worked on the screen, ignoring the notification in lieu of calling the one person who would have the balls to download an app like this onto his phone.

It was nearly midnight on a Friday.

He didn't give a shit.

It rang twice, three times, and then Claire picked up. "Hello?"

Music blared in the background, a thumping bass told him his assistant had more of a social life than he did, and maybe he was an asshole for calling her at midnight on a Friday.

But in that moment, he didn't care.

In that moment, he was tempted to fire her.

Which would make his life a fucking nightmare because she was the best person he'd ever hired.

"You downloaded *Tinder*?" he snapped.

Silence.

Well, silence from the woman, not silence from the background. The bass still thumped, and the noise was intense, so much so that even though he kept the phone a few inches from his ear, he could still hear it.

Same as he could hear her shouted out, "You need to get laid!"

Now, it was his turn for a blip of silence, before he snapped, "I'm your boss, for Christ's sake!"

This time, she didn't miss a beat. "You're my boss, who'll be a better boss if you get laid," she said. "So, consider it my civic duty or office duty or . . . whatever, consider it my duty to humanity to get you a woman so that you can fucking relax."

The balls on this one.

"I should fire you right now."

"Except you won't," Claire said. "Because I'm the shit, and you couldn't survive without me."

Unfortunately, she was right.

"So, enjoy the kickass profile I put together and get swiping. Find some way"—a hint of humor in her tone—"or rather, some*one* to take the edge off."

Then she hung up.

Hung. Up.

On him. Her boss. The CEO of the company that would set her up for life.

If she didn't get her ass fired.

His phone buzzed.

You're not going to fire me.

Ben narrowed his eyes at the text as another came through.

Now unwind a little. God knows you deserve it.

He kept his eyes narrowed. More buzzing commenced.

I know it's inappropriate, but I love you and care about you.

His glare relaxed, and his fingers moved on the screen.

Fine. You're not fired.

A beat. Then, his phone vibrated again—

I love you too, Claire. That's what you're supposed to say.

That wasn't something he was capable of saying. Not any longer. Which, aside from him working nearly every waking moment, was probably why he was single. All the money in the world couldn't overcome the fact that he didn't have it in him to love anymore.

Sighing, he dropped his phone to the couch cushion, thanking God that it didn't buzz again.

Claire would get back to her night.

He would risk Sweetheart's snarling and get another beer.

Then tomorrow, he'd get back to work. Implement phase two of Hunt Inc.

Because work was all he was capable of. That was it, and

anyone who thought that he might be able to give anything more than that was just going to be disappointed in him.

But even with knowing all that . . .

For some reason, he picked up his phone.

And he opened the app.

CHAPTER FIVE

Stef

SHE LOVED SAN FRANCISCO.

She loved her friends—well, the ones she'd made in the last six months, not the jerkwads who'd abandoned her after she and Jeremy had broken up.

Heidi and company were the best. Even if they did get her drunk.

Okay, that was part of the reason they were wonderful.

Also, she loved margaritas. Also, she'd finished the remnants of the sweet and sour drink from the blender, and now she had decided she was *really* in love with margaritas. And her friends. And San Francisco.

And especially in love with the squishy, floating feeling that had invaded her limbs.

What she *didn't* love?

The lack of sex in her life.

Sure, she had her drawer of friendly vibrators, but . . . it wasn't the same.

Okay, sometimes it was *better*. Especially compared to Jeremy and his incompetent penis.

But oftentimes her vibrator time was . . . well, a bit lacking. She wanted more than just a cock. She wanted a hot, hard, strong body poised on top of her. She wanted a man to pick her up and pin her to a wall, pounding deep and hard and—

Hard.

The trouble was that there weren't a lot of men who were interested in a frumpy scientist who had an obsession with *Stargate.*

Especially when her friends had taken all the good men.

"Bitches," she muttered.

Which was why she was lying in bed, wearing her favorite cozy pajamas and trying to work up the urge to . . . swipe right.

Because the man on the app was gorgeous.

When she'd first seen him, her vagina had jumped up, doing a happy dance—complete with pasties and sparklers and a skimpy thong. Well, not so much skimpy because skimpy and her body type didn't mix, but she'd at least slip into some high-cut bikini bottoms, and she'd *definitely* shave her legs.

Maybe her armpits, too.

He was so worth an extended shower and using her expensive soap and spending an hour blow-drying her thick-ass hair.

He would be worth Spanx and lace and—

"Just do it," she whispered.

But the problem with swiping right was that this beautiful man with the sexiest smile she'd ever laid eyes on would invariably swipe left on her picture, and she'd still be here, lying in bed, in her pajamas, and reaching for her vibrator instead of the man himself.

And Fred would be locked in his crate, judging her for getting herself off. *Again.*

But she couldn't flick the bean with her dog in bed next to her.

That was just . . .

She shuddered.

It was also . . . not the point. The *point* being that she was single, and she was horny, and she was drunk.

So drunk. *So* horny. *So* alone.

Le sigh.

That picture called to her again, her thumb hovered over the screen, so close to swiping—

"No," she muttered. "*No* men."

Men were untrustworthy fuckers, who brought unnecessary complications.

Despite their hard cocks that could occasionally bring her to orgasm.

"Ugh."

She tossed her phone on the mattress, hit play on her show, and settled in with her glass of wine (thanks to her hidden stash that her friends hadn't found, ha!) and her sexy, just as fictional as the man in the app, Colonel Jack O'Neill.

See?

Her life was full.

She had good friends. She had good vibrators. She had a good job.

She had a *great* dog.

"I don't need anything else, do I, Fred?"

Her fluffy friend, with his adorable golden retriever face and his fuzzy tail, glanced up at her, tail thumping on the mattress. Yeah, no. No orgasm was worth locking him in his kennel. He was exhausted after a long day of doggy day care, the excitement of her friends coming over, and currently curled up in the space where her imaginary man might reside.

Another *see?*

Because she didn't have room for the app man, any more than she had room for that fictional colonel.

It was her and Fred and her bottle of wine.

That was good enough.

Except . . . it *wasn't* good enough when she finished her episode and went to the kitchen for another bottle of wine, letting the show continue to play. It *wasn't* good enough when she finished that wine over another episode, and her mind got thinking again, only this time swirling because she was plumb full of wine, of margaritas.

It wasn't good enough when her reserve disappeared into the wind, and she used her drunk coordination to pick up her cell, her lack of inhibition to . . . swipe right.

Bleary eyes shutting, she let her arm drop to the bed, the phone slipping out of her grip, sleep claiming her fast and heavily.

And in the morning, *SG-1* still rolling on autoplay, when her headache and hangover meant that she'd almost forgotten about the fictional man and her drunk swiping . . .

In the morning, she woke up, peeled back her lids, squinted with bleary eyes, and saw—

He'd swiped right, too.

Oh, fuck.

CHAPTER SIX

Ben

HE'D EXPECTED AN IMMEDIATE RESPONSE.

He'd seen the red lips, the shoulder-length brown hair, the brown eyes that on first glance looked open and happy, but on closer inspection, held a slice of sad.

That sad had called to something inside him.

The eight beers he'd consumed, probably.

But still, he'd ignored everything in him telling him to delete the app, to ignore the woman, to ignore the fire that had begun burning in his gut when he'd seen the sad, and he'd swiped right.

And then he'd expected something to happen.

Instead, he'd gotten a screen telling him he had a match and then . . . nothing.

Now, there was still no response, it was morning and for some fucking reason, he was Googling what he should do after a match and realizing that he probably needed to be the one to take that first step. Which meant he was currently neck-deep in online advice telling him to send a message with everything from "Hey" to snapping a picture of his dick and texting it to her.

The first didn't seem like enough.

The last seemed like a surefire way to get blocked and ruin any chance of tasting those pretty red lips.

So, now he'd opened up the message center and was staring blankly at the box he should be filling with words, with a pithy joke or pickup line, and was back to contemplating deleting the app again, just to put himself out of his misery.

Then his phone pinged.

With a message from her. From Stef McKay.

Hey.

She got to just say *hey?*

Seriously?

What the fuck was that bullshit?

Well, two could play that game. His fingers worked on the phone screen, sent those same three letters back.

Hey.

Take that. Back in her court, Ms. Stef McKay.

Then he realized he was being an idiot and knew he should be saying something else. This was basically a business deal. A transaction that would get them both something mutually satisfactory.

If he looked at it that way, all would be good.

Nodding to himself, he took off his fucking horrible with women hat and put on his business one, and then typed out a message.

You have a nice smile.

Pedestrian.

But a compliment, especially one that wasn't about her tits (which looked nice from the small glimpse of cleavage in her profile pic) or ass (which he hoped was lush, also based on the curves in her photo), so he figured it was a step up from *hey*.

A moment later, she replied.

You have nice eyes.

He grinned, the compliment flowing over him like warm water. Maybe this online dating thing wasn't so hard.

Except . . . what did he say now? Another compliment, but would that be trying too hard? Should he ask her about work? Or would that come off as creepy, trying to get too much information when they'd just matched on an app and didn't know each other?

Hobbies!

He should ask her about her hobbies.

Quickly, he navigated to her profile, saw a line in the description that said, *Science geek. Golden Retriever lover. Wars over Trek.*

The first and the last made him smile—the last especially—but he didn't know if it was one of those things that women just said, trying to be all nerdy cute. Her picture certainly didn't scream nerd in any way. But paired with the first, he felt a sliver of heat slide through him.

Damn. He needed to search up some science facts to impress her.

Except, what kind of science?

It was kind of a vast area of study, and . . . now he was overthinking this.

He'd stick with the dog. They at least had that in common, although he wouldn't go so far as to say that he was a Sweetheart Lover.

Okay. Dogs.

You like Golden Retrievers?

He sent after navigating back to their chat.
Barely a few seconds before she responded. With a picture.

My Fred.

A hairy face. Friendly eyes. A tongue hanging out that would probably drool all over Ben's expensive shoes. And the fucker was adorable. Not the evil and potential violence of Sweetheart, the I'm-gonna-cut-you-bitch gleaming black eyes.

He's cute. I wrote. *Why Fred?*

Another message came through.

Why not *Fred?*

There was that.

You make a good point.

Her reply came in just a few heartbeats.

Wow. A man who can admit that. Have I stumbled upon a Unicorn?

His brows were drawn together.

A unicorn?

A buzz.

No. Not a unicorn, *but rather a Unicorn. Capital U.*

Um. Okay . . .

Her next reply came, thankfully, before he'd been required to come up with a reply for that.

You like dogs.

Well, now, that wasn't phrased as a question, so he just let it lie there, not touching it, not revealing too much. He hadn't let himself think too much about the things he liked or didn't like, and he didn't think the red-lipped, curved beauty would think much of *him* if he admitted that his dog-liking capabilities fell more into the realm of dog-tolerating.

Instead, he sent,

What kind of science are you a geek about?

This pause was a bit longer.

Physics.

His brows lifted.

Physics? That's impressive. I nearly failed that class in college.

It was the single science class he'd been required to take for his business degree, and no joke, it had nearly killed him. He'd been thrilled to just pass with a C—the only C he'd received in all his advanced studies.

A bachelor's. Two master's.

School had been important to his parents and to him.

But thank fuck business administration and management hadn't required a second round of physics.

Too bad I wasn't around to tutor you. I wouldn't have let you fail, nearly or otherwise.

He knew he would have studied until he passed out if Stef had been his tutor and then probably died for another reason—if one could die of blue balls. Because if he found himself taciturn and withdrawn now, he'd been cripplingly shy in his younger years.

Nose in a book.

Gangly as fuck.

All the way up until his dad had died, and then the fury had taken over. He'd been pissed to lose him, pissed that his mom was devastated, pissed that the world had lost the one person he thought deserved to live over everyone else.

Ben's dad had been good.

So fucking good.

And he'd died for absolutely no reason. Same as his mom. Fucking cancer. Fucking people who just wanted something that didn't belong to him. Fucking . . .

World.

He'd hit the gym after his dad died. Hadn't stopped through his mom's illness, the cancer having been found just months after they had put his dad in the ground. And it had crept through her, taking her strength, her hair, her eyelashes, and finally, her life.

So, sometimes he wanted to go punish something, and he did that to a punching bag. Sometimes he wanted to punish himself, which he did running and lifting until he could barely move the next day.

Now, at least, he wasn't scrawny.

But he still hadn't mastered the art of talking to women.

Case in point, what happened next. Ben sent,

Do you want to grab a coffee?

Then waited for her to reply.

And waited a little longer.

Then still longer.

Or not, he typed. *If you're not comfortable.*

His pulse thrummed as he held his breath, waiting, but after long minutes without her responding, Ben knew he'd fucked up. Pressed too soon, asked her before she was ready. "Fuck," he muttered, tossing his cell on his nightstand and shoving himself out of bed.

Coffee had been the wrong move.

But seriously, this was why he stayed in his world. Because business negotiations were less complicated than women. Maybe he should have doled out another compliment, stuck with asking her something about herself, about fucking physics, rather than moving straight to asking her out.

She probably thought he just wanted to get laid.

Which, yes, that *was* his intention.

But he knew better—or at least he *should* know that this type of thing needed finesse.

He might as well have sent a dick pic.

Sighing, he cranked on the shower and set about getting ready for the day. He'd go into the office, get started on phase two for Hunt Inc. He wanted to go global, and in order to do that, he'd need to make sure all his plans for expansion were in place.

And to do that, he needed to focus on work.

So, he was done thinking about women with sexy red lips and a glimpse of curves he wanted to get his hands on.

Even if that glimpse had him wrapping his fingers around his cock and stroking as the water sluiced down his spine, as the release built up.

This was just as good as a woman.

He didn't need red lips.

Or breasts.

Or an ass to grab on to as he pumped into her pussy, deep and slow and steady. She'd be tight. She'd grind back against him, and—

"Fuck," he groaned, slamming his hand against the tile as he came.

Imagining red lips.

Imagining curves.

Imagining . . . Stef McKay.

And knowing his hand wouldn't be anything when compared to her.

CHAPTER SEVEN

Stef

Do you want to grab a coffee?

SUCH A SIMPLE QUESTION.

An easy yes or no . . . and in this case, it should most definitely be a yes. Because Ben Bradford was gorgeous, and he'd said he liked her smile, and he hadn't sent her a picture of his cock or asked her to meet up to fuck without any fluff.

He'd asked her to coffee.

And she'd launched her phone across the room in a fit of panic, startling Fred awake. Which had led to her pupper needing to get pottied and fed *right* then. Which was fine, because she couldn't look at that message and not start thinking about what in the fuck she had been doing to have swiped on the sexy Denzel in his younger days, cropped hair, stubbled jaw, deep, beautiful eyes man who'd come across her feed.

She was short and stout—

Like a fucking teapot.

Her hair was mud colored. Her eyes were fine, albeit a boring brown. Her skin was nice, if someone liked the nearly see-through version of white of someone who worked in a lab all day and rarely saw the sun—unless it was on beach day, and then that was as the sun was going down, so it didn't do much to add any color.

She didn't match with a man like Ben, even if an app had let her pretend that might be the case, just for a minute.

So, she'd left her cell in the corner of the room, had let Fred into the back yard for a few minutes so he could do his business, and then set about making his brekkie, with his vitamins and his shredded chicken and his super expensive kibble.

Then she fed her boy, showered, and she set about planning her meals for the week, just like she did every Saturday.

She went to the farmer's market, the grocery store. She chopped and threw chicken in the Crock-Pot and prepped her lunches for the week, using some of that chicken but saving most of it for Fred and his meals. While doing all that, she watched a couple of episodes of a promising new superhero show on Netflix, knowing she'd complete the eight-part binge that evening.

After beach time.

And beach time was glorious.

Beach time was beautiful, the perfect mix of late afternoon sunshine and early evening breeze, the stars just beginning to shine.

Fred was exhausted when they returned, having just barely summoned the energy to eat before putting himself in his crate, a rare occurrence that illustrated exactly how much fun her little man had had splashing in the waves.

So now, she was eating a salad and eyeing her phone.

Do you want to get a coffee?

She did. Stef wanted that. *Bad.* And that was what fucking terrified her. Because she'd barely recovered from Jeremy, and Jeremy had been an asshole. Ben Bradford might turn out to be an asshole, too, but he'd complimented her smile, and Jeremy had never done that, never complimented much about her, and certainly not just out of the blue. To avoid a fight? Oh yeah. To get laid? Certainly. But just something nice without being prompted? No, not that she could think of. All of which said something sad about her, something that she didn't want to keep considering because it illustrated exactly how pathetic she'd been to waste her time with Jeremy.

Had he ever liked her?

Like at all?

Or had she been convenient and allowed herself to be a punching bag?

He must have been nice in the beginning. He had to have been. Right? Except . . . she couldn't think of any examples, and that just made her feel worse about herself.

Which . . . seriously, how was that possible?

More than six months of pretending to be fine about the breakup while knowing that she hadn't been fine before, hadn't been fine while they were together.

But she was going to be fine.

And she was also kidding herself if she thought that Ben didn't have an ulterior motive. He wasn't looking for love. Just like Jeremy, he wanted to bone and then go on with his life.

Tell me how you know that.

Why—seriously, fucking *why*—did every second guess she had of herself come in the form of her mom's voice? Always chastising and disapproving. Always making her second-guess what she was doing.

Fuck.

"Enough," she murmured. "Just enough."

That was a sufficient amount of self-reflection and pitying for the evening. She needed to go back to what she did best— looking forward, picking up, and moving on. She'd done it when her brother had been sick, so sick, so troubled, struggling so *fucking* much, that she'd basically been on her own. Alone, even amongst her family, she'd needed to live her own life. She'd done it when he'd taken his own life and her parents had needed someone to pick up the pieces and move everyone on.

But she'd spent too long picking up the pieces for everyone else.

Now, she needed to pick them up, only for herself this time.

That was why she left her phone in the corner of the room, the battery slowly draining, while she and Fred finished bingeing that superhero show.

CHAPTER EIGHT

Ben, Three Months Later

HE RAN a hand over his head, feeling the bristles of his hair against his palm, knowing he needed a haircut, yet not wanting to take the time to bother.

Hunt Inc. was firmly in phase two.

He'd worked himself to exhaustion every night for the last few months. The company's stock was up. He'd never been more productive.

But he couldn't stop jacking off to red lips and deep brown eyes.

His cock twitched.

"Fuck," he muttered, tossing the file he'd been reading onto his desk, just as there was a perfunctory knock at the door and Claire stuck her head in the opening.

"Do I need to escort you down to your car?" she said, leaning a hip against the doorframe. "Or are you going to leave at a reasonable hour for the first time in an eternity?"

Ben sighed, considered telling her to piss off, or maybe threatening to fire her again. But that never worked, and frankly, he didn't have the energy for it.

Not today.

Not on *this* day.

He'd put his mom in the ground exactly one year before.

"Ben?" Claire asked, the sass leaving her tone, worry taking its place. "You okay?"

He blinked, pushed to his feet, and reached into the top drawer of his desk to retrieve his wallet. "I'm out of here."

"You are?" she asked, shifting to the side when he approached the door. "Really?"

"It's Friday," he told her. "Why don't you take off early, too?"

Her brows lifted before she lifted her wrist and glanced at her watch. "Early meaning eight-thirty?"

Shit. Was it already eight-thirty?

He glanced out the windows, saw that it was dark. Ah. Yeah, it was.

"Okay," he amended. "Why don't you get out of here now?"

"That's the plan." She followed him toward the elevator after briefly asking, "You want to come out with us?"

He snorted. "You want to drink a beer with your boss?"

She glanced up at him as they stepped onto the elevator. "You realize we've been friends for near on a decade," she said. "Just because I'm your assistant—"

"Should I point out that you're my assistant because you refused my offer to be VP?"

She made a face. "I don't have the requisite fancy letters after my name to take that position," she muttered, hitting the button to take them down to the garage. "I didn't even finish high school, for God's sake."

Ben covered her hand with his. "You're the smartest person I know. Bar none."

A scoff, her fingers slipping from his. "So says the boy genius."

He rolled his eyes. "So says your *boss*, who's not going to hire another VP because I expect your ass to be in that office come Monday morning."

"You won't be able to get through your day without me."

That was the worst part of offering Claire the position. He'd be out the best assistant in his crew. But also, he wouldn't be the person who was going to hold her back, and God knew he should have made this move for her years ago.

She knew every role in the company, had worked every job, had been his right hand from the moment he'd started the business. His first employee. His friend.

"You're right," he said. "But I'll have Spence and Baine and even though I won't have another Claire, I'll be happy because I know that you'll be where you should be."

"You'll be miserable."

"That, too." He shrugged, not bothering to hide his smile. "Except, I also know that you'll have a replacement ready for me on Monday, and you'll train him or her up so he or she will be a mini-Claire before long."

She made a face.

He shrugged again. "You're only mad because you know it's true."

The elevator doors opened with a ding, and they stepped off, this time with Claire glaring up at him. "Only because I don't want to hear you bitch about how incompetent your new assistant is, over and *over* again."

"I don't bitch about Spence and Baine."

"Not anymore." A beat. "And only because Baine is training Spence."

He rolled his eyes. "I'm not *that* bad."

She just looked at him.

"Okay, fine," Ben muttered. "But it's not a bad thing to like things the way I like them."

Claire smirked. "You're a boring stick in the mud."

Since that much was true, he didn't bother arguing.

"Stick. In. The. Mud."

He rolled his eyes. "*Claire.*"

"You deleted the app, didn't you?" she asked, as he walked her to her car. "Without even bothering to match with anyone."

No. He hadn't deleted the app.

He'd left it on his phone, buried in a folder, and occasionally opened the message chain and called himself a moron. And then he'd scroll to that profile, to that picture, to those red lips.

And he'd want to get *Moron* tattooed on his forehead.

"I don't have time to date."

"So, you're just going to work nonstop for another eight years, let the world pass you by, and not have anything on the other side of it?"

"Not nothing," he said, tugging open the door for her. "I have you."

Claire's lips pressed flat. "I'm dating someone."

This made his brows raise. "Is it serious?"

She grinned. "No."

He snorted. "Then I've still got my fabulous new VP."

Quiet, amusement drifting across her face. "That you do."

"Yeah?" he asked, fighting a smile at the first sign of her agreeing to take the positon.

Another grin. "Yeah."

Ben leaned down and kissed her cheek. "That's better than a match any day of the week."

Her expression went soft. "Ben—"

He straightened. "See you Monday."

Then he closed her door, moved to his own car, and drove home.

Because, between then and Monday, he'd do what he did best.

Work.

CHAPTER NINE

Stef

SHE WAS BORDERING ON BUZZED.

Margaritas for the win, but this time of the prickly pear variety.

They were eating at their favorite Mexican place, and while they usually met on Thursdays, this week Stef, Tammy, Cora, and the Couples, as they'd termed the other non-single women and their partners in their friend group, had gotten together on Friday.

They had chips and fajitas and prickly pear margaritas.

And fun.

Lots and lots of fun.

But even though it was tempting to dive into the newest pitcher of margaritas, she was tired. It had been a long week, and Fred had woken her up early that morning. She knew that if she had another glass, she was going to be straight buzzed, and then she wouldn't be driving home.

She'd need a ride to the restaurant in the morning, and her chores and errands would start last. Which meant beach day would probably be delayed, and . . . Fred would unhappy.

Which meant *she* would be unhappy.

Because the little—big—fuzz bucket would probably take his unhappiness out on her sock drawer.

And she wasn't willing to give up a single pair of them.

So she had cut herself off, was eating her homemade tortillas like a champ, and going to make sure her buzz trickled away so she could drive safely home to her little Freddy-bear.

Grinning to herself, she scooped up an obscene amount of salsa onto a chip and crammed it into her mouth. Then another tortilla. Then more peppers and onions and steak and salsa and chips until she felt like she was bursting from all the food. Only then did she look up and see the entire table staring at her. "What?" she asked, and so yeah, maybe it was muffled from the remnants of a chip in her mouth.

Tanner's brows lifted, his gaze turning to Kelsey. "Should I check and see if the kitchen has any food left?"

Stef glared.

Kels popped him on the shoulder. "Rude much?"

"The girl just hoovered everything on the table," he said. "I don't think that I'm rude, so much as impressed. Where does she put it all?"

Now Stef rolled her eyes. "It's her fault," she mumbled after chewing and swallowing, pointing at Heidi. "She works me to the bone, night and day."

Heidi gasped. "How dare you?"

"How dare *I?*" Stef teased. "I'm not the one who ate *my* lunch."

Narrowed eyes, even as the table broke out into laughter mixed with admonishments. "That was one time," Heidi said. "And it was an accident."

Stef smirked. "An accident that you ate the whole thing?"

Heidi blushed.

"I'm just saying, I'm not the only one who can eat." She pointed at the table, where the rest of them had gone to town on their own plates. "And also, I like salsa too much to give a shit about the fact that I'm carrying a taco baby around."

Click.

She blinked at the flash, the sound of Tanner taking a photograph.

"Sorry," Tanner said, setting his camera on the table. "You're beautiful."

It wasn't a come-on, or weird—or not that much anyway. Tanner was a photographer. World-famous, supremely talented. People paid boatloads of money to get him to take their picture.

But he took a lot of photos of everyone when they were all together, and they were fabulous.

Including, she saw when she gestured for the camera and he handed it over, glancing at the screen on the back, the one he'd just taken of her.

If Stef hadn't been looking at herself, she would have agreed the woman in the photograph was beautiful. Fierce eyes, a flush on her cheeks, hair shining from the lights overhead. There was fire in her, even though she'd been yelling about food and taco babies.

It was . . . nice to see the fire again.

"Okay?" Tanner asked, squatting next to her and sliding the camera from her hands. He glanced at her face and winced. "Never mind, I'll delete it."

"No," she said, covering his fingers with her own. "It's . . . will you send it to me?"

His face gentled. "Of course." A beat. "And for the record, I wasn't trying to make fun of you, I *was* truly impressed." A grin. "From one Hoover to the next."

Laughing, she nudged his shoulder. "Speaking of which, you'd better go eat up before I take care of business for you."

A grin. "Noted."

She glanced up, saw Kels smiling apologetically, but Stef just shook her head, letting her friend know she was in on the joke and happy with the picture, even if it felt a bit like Tanner was their own paparazzo.

Still, it was nice to have the moments documented.

She didn't have many pictures of herself.

She wasn't really into selfies, and Jeremy certainly hadn't taken many of her, and her parents . . . well, sometimes things slipped through the cracks when a family was just trying to survive.

Tammy nudged her arm. "You okay, bugaboo?"

Stef's brows lifted. "Bugaboo?"

"Ignore me." Tammy's cheeks went a little pink. "As much as I want to not be like my mother, she still creeps in sometimes."

"That's not a bad thing," Stef told her. "I've met your mom, and she's great."

A sigh. "She *is* great," Tammy agreed, sadness flickering behind her pale brown eyes. "But try living in the shadow of all that greatness."

Stef knew something about shadows, something she'd shared the barest of details with her friends. *Something* that Tammy obviously remembered because she reached over and grabbed Stef's hand. "Shit," she said. "I'm sorry."

"Hey." Stef nudged her shoulder, squeezed back. "We're not in a one-upmanship trauma contest. If it hurt your heart, you don't get to discount it." She smiled. "You can move past it, but you don't get to discount it. It's part of you and important and—"

She broke off.

"Sorry," she murmured. "This is too serious of a conversation for prickly pear margaritas."

On that note, she decided to fuck it all, tugged her hand from Tammy's, and poured herself another margarita.

A Lyft it would be.

Fred would just have to deal.

Tammy's fingers brushed the back of Stef's. "You're an

amazing woman," she said, and Stef forced herself to accept the compliment, to not snort and discount it like her first instinct pressed her to do.

"Thank you," Stef murmured. "You are, too."

Tammy grinned. "I wasn't done, you know?"

"Done with what?" Heidi asked, her focus drawn from across the table to their conversation.

"Done with complimenting Stef and watching her squirm because she doesn't believe them," Tammy said.

"Oh!" Heidi clapped her hands together. "I like this game."

Stef groaned, began sucking back her margarita.

"She's brilliant," Heidi said. "My lab wouldn't run nearly as efficiently without her."

Another groan, her head falling to the table.

Kate laughed, drawing Stef's focus. "I'd add kind to that list." A smile. "And a great baker." She rubbed her stomach. "Based on the dozen muffins I ate last time you brought them to our house."

"And didn't share," Jaime, her husband, added with a wink. Kate narrowed her eyes, but Jaime just smoothed her hair back, kissed her cheek, and then turned back to Stef. "My addition to the list is that she's a great dog mom."

Okay, now her heart was melting. Because Jaime was Jaime the Vet, and knowing that he approved of her dog mom skills meant a lot.

Her Fred was a special boy.

"Thanks, Jaime."

He winked, snagged a pepper from Kate's plate.

"Are we going around the table?" Brad asked, his eyes—a slightly deeper brown than his brother's—sparkling with humor.

"God, no," Stef muttered.

"Yes!" Cora said. "She has great taste in nerd. *Stargate-SG1* is the shit."

"Oh, Lord," Stef moaned, dropping her head to the table

again. But only for a moment, because Cora tugged her up and shoved her glass in her hand.

"Drink and absorb," she ordered.

Drink. Oh, she'd *drink* all right. She glugged down that margarita, refilled her glass, and continued shoveling in chips and salsa.

"Great," Brad said. "I'll go next."

She clenched her teeth together, met his gaze when he waited for her to meet his eyes, all the aplomb of a magician gathering his audience's attention. "I'd second the good baker" —a pat to his belly—"and good dog mom."

Her cheeks blazed.

"That Fred, even with his obsession with squirrels, is a good boy."

"He is," she murmured.

He grinned. "But I'd say, more than that, you're a good friend, and we're all lucky to have you in our lives."

Not, the girls were lucky to have her.

But *all* of them.

She sniffed.

All the women sniffed.

"How the hell am I supposed to follow that?" Kels grumbled, even as Stef was thinking *how in the hell was she supposed to act like this was all normal when she felt like her heart was going to explode out of her chest?*

Meanwhile, Tanner said, "I'll just reiterate *beautiful.*"

Silence.

Then more sniffing.

Cora whispered, "All the good men." A beat. "The bitches have taken them all."

Stef sighed, even though they were both smiling. Because fucking hell, she was right. "I know," she muttered and turned to Tammy. "How in the hell are you supposed to date someone and not compare them to those jokers?"

Tammy shook her head, ponytail fluttering behind her. "I

don't date." A shrug. "So, the problem is solved." Her lips twitched. "No comparisons necessary."

"Probably for the best," Stef said, reaching for her glass again.

She held it up, touched it to Tammy's.

"To margaritas over men."

Tammy grinned, tapped back. "To margaritas over men."

CHAPTER TEN

Ben

His phone buzzed when he was debating getting up and going to bed.

He picked it up off the table, expecting to see a text but instead heat trailed down his spine and red lips flashed to the forefront of his mind.

Holding his breath, he opened the app.

I'm sorry I didn't reply.

Shock washed over him, and he found his fingers moving without thinking.

Why didn't you?

Silence.

No response for long minutes.

His gut sank, and he tossed his phone on the table. He needed to delete the fucking app and just be done with it.

Sweetheart snarled as he flopped back on the couch—well,

more grumble than growl. Things between them had improved, mostly because he'd stopped trying to get pet sitters and had just been bringing the princess into the office with him every day.

He, apparently, was the least unpleasant scenario.

It might also be that him bringing her to his office every day meant that she could growl at him at will.

His phone buzzed again, surprising the hell out of him.

I was scared.

Ben read those three words and came to the obvious conclusion. He was a Black guy. She was a white girl. *Of course*, she was scared of him. It fucking sucked, but it wasn't the first time he'd gotten that reaction, and no doubt it wouldn't be the last. It just . . . hurt.

This time, he was the one who didn't respond.

He dropped his phone back on the table and went into the bathroom, brushing his teeth, washing his face, going to bed . . . except, he needed to charge his phone. And that was the only reason he went back to the family room and picked up his cell.

The *only* reason.

But when he happened to glance at the screen—happened to see the open app—he saw that it was filled with messages.

I was scared because you're beautiful. The most beautiful man I've ever seen. And I'm just me, whose boyfriend broke up with her because she was boring.

And also maybe because I loved my dog more than him.

You're mysterious and sexy and have amazing eyes and stubble and . . . I usually spend my nights watching Stargate while reading research papers.

You asked me to coffee and I panicked and I shouldn't be typing this.

But I'm drunk and waiting for my Lyft and . . . shit. I know I shouldn't be typing this.

So why can't I stop?

Right.

Because I'm drunk and my Lyft doesn't appear to be coming.

So I'm going to request another one, save you from my drunk ass, and go back to not messaging you.

Not that you'll do anything but block me after this.

Or not respond. Because I deserve that.

Anyway, goodbye, Ben. Sorry I ghosted you before.

He reached the end of that text diarrhea to find his heart pounding, hope he was trying to ignore blossoming inside him.

Because she was drunk and waiting for a ride, who knew where, and he shouldn't give a fuck, but his gut was twisting itself into knots thinking of red lips and curves being out there and drunk and . . . vulnerable.

Where are you?

He sent it and when she didn't immediately respond, he sent another message.

Stef, honey, where are you right now?

A few seconds, his stomach clenched tight, before she replied.

Bobby's Bar. My friends and I went for drinks after dinner.

Relief coursed through him.

You're not alone then? They'll get you home?

A long pause.

I put them in their Lyft. Waiting for mine.

"Fuck," he hissed, shoving his feet into his shoes and shrugging into his jacket.

How long?

He moved out his front door, down the elevator to the garage.

For what?

Clamping the phone into the holder perched in his air vent, he replied before backing out of the stall.

Until the Lyft comes.

He was already on the freeway when she replied.

Don't worry about it.

Fucking hell. He pulled over, typed a message, then continued driving.

How long?

A long pause, long enough that Ben's teeth felt as though they'd been ground down to their nubs. Then her response came through, and it made pain radiate down his jaw.

It's surging. Still trying to match.

He pulled in a breath through his nose, glad that he was only a few minutes out, and released it slowly as he exited the freeway and paused at the signal at the bottom of the off-ramp.

Risking a ticket, he speed-typed then continued driving.

I'll be there in five minutes.

Nothing.

Then a flurry of messages came through.

He caught one of them as he stopped at a stop sign, but then he was continuing to drive, nearing the entrance of Bobby's and slowing, looking for curves and red lips and . . .

There.

Shorter than he'd expected.

An ass that looked glorious in a pair of jeans. He'd known. He'd *known*.

Carefully, he pulled up to the curb and rolled down the window. "Stef."

Her eyes were wide, and when he said her name, she squeaked. Literally squeaked. Fuck, she was cute. He put on the flashers and got out, rounding the hood and stopping in front of her.

Freckles.

She had a swathe of freckles on her nose.

Her hair was pulled back into a low ponytail, a few whisps having escaped to frame her face. "Get in," he said. "I'll drive you home."

"You're here," she breathed, lifting her hand up as though she'd stroke his jaw. But her fingers halted, just before she touched him, near enough that he could actually feel the heat from them on his skin.

Then she skittered back a step.

"You're *here?*" Her mouth opened and closed a few times. "But why are you here?"

He glanced over his shoulder. "I need to move my car. You getting in, so I can drive you home?"

Her teeth nibbled on her bottom lip.

"Not a serial killer," he said. "I promise. You can call your friends and stay on the line with them on the way, if that makes you feel better."

She still nibbled.

He bit back a sigh. "I'll park and wait until your Lyft gets here." Ben turned back to his car and started to get in. He'd seen a spot just around the corner.

"Why are you here, Ben?"

The sound of his name in her voice, a little huskier than he'd expected, made a shiver skate down his spine. His nostrils flared. "You said you were drunk and without a ride. I needed . . ."

Her eyes widened, and she stepped closer. "Needed what?" she breathed.

"To make sure you got home safe," he snapped, glaring at the people gathered in front of the bar, coupled off and talking or kissing, the shadows where who knew what threat lurked.

"I'm perfectly capable of getting home."

"You *said* you were drunk." A beat. "And alone."

Her mouth hitched up. Then she patted his arm, brushed by him, and got into his car.

The slam of the door startled him out of his shock, and he spun, got into the driver's seat, and pulled down the street, navigating his way back to the freeway. "Where to?" he asked, when he realized he didn't know which direction to go.

She gave him directions, a far sight south of the bar, south of his place in the city.

"You don't seem very drunk," he said after a few moments.

Stef rolled her head on the seat, turning to look at him. He saw that her pupils were wide and dark pools in the moonlight before he forced his eyes back to the road. "It's just—" She broke off, was quiet for long enough that he wanted to press, but then she spoke again. "I'm really good at faking I'm okay." Then just as quickly as that admission came, she cleared her throat, looked back at the road, and her voice went chipper. "But I couldn't drive home, anyway. My car is at the restaurant we ate dinner at." She named a popular Mexican place in the area.

"I see."

He didn't see.

Not at all.

But her lips were painted red, her curves were in the seat next to him, and he had a long drive ahead of them.

All of a sudden, his night was looking up.

CHAPTER ELEVEN

Stef

SHE STILL HAD a lovely floaty feeling, but she knew that her being in this car wasn't her drunk mind hallucinating.

Ben was here.

He'd come because he was worried she was sloppy and on the street without a safe way to get home.

Her heart was . . . vulnerable.

Oh boy, *was* it vulnerable.

Her kryptonite was someone taking care of her, looking out for her without her asking. Without her begging.

And even her margarita brain could recognize that it was a weakness, that it was stupid to have gotten in a car with a man she didn't know, to give him her address, to have drunk messaged him in the first place.

Stupid. So stupid.

Except . . . his eyes.

They were gentle, and then he'd told her to call a friend and stay on the line while he drove, and a muscle in his jaw had ticked, and she'd wanted to stroke the muscle twitching in that jaw, to feel the bristles on her fingertips.

And he'd gone out of his way to come help her.

So, here she was. In the passenger seat of a sleek sports car, its engine rumbling beneath her as he drove through the night. It was clear, the moon bright and gleaming, the fog having stayed curled over the ocean, not invading inland yet. That fog would probably creep inward at some point, but for right now, she was enjoying the gleam of the moon, casting everything in silver.

"Thank you," she murmured. "You didn't have to do this."

"It's nothing."

Not to her.

So she said, "Not to me." And then she said something that she certainly wouldn't have said if she'd been stone-cold sober, something she would have been too tongue-tied to say without alcohol. "I don't want to go home yet."

His gaze drifted to hers again. "Where do you want to go?"

She shrugged.

Quiet then, "I know a place."

She inhaled sharply. She should tell him to forget it, to take her home, to forget about this and her drunk message and her fantasies. Because her heart was vulnerable, and if he continued being nice, then she was going to fall for him.

Just like she'd fallen for Jeremy.

And look how that turned out.

But instead, she asked, "What kind of place?"

"A quiet one."

Her lips twitched. "Where you can pull out those serial killer skills?"

He chuckled, and the sound rolled over her, warm fingers trailing over her skin. "Quiet, but not private. Plenty of people around to keep those in check."

Stef's brows drew together, confusion and curiosity threading through her. "Is it an orgy?" she asked suspiciously, though not realizing until after it was out there that an orgy probably wouldn't be quiet.

Ben was, though.

Until he burst out laughing, and then *that* sound was warm, like rough palms on her naked skin, a hard cock between her thighs, sliding home. She shifted on her seat, legs pressing together, heat making her pussy slick.

"Not an orgy," he murmured.

But he wouldn't be opposed to it? her brain helpfully chimed in.

Or unhelpfully? Because Ben was wearing a tight navy T-shirt and gray sweats that clung to powerful thighs. His biceps were solid, his shoulders broad and something she could grab on to.

He might be the sexiest man she had ever seen.

No, he *was* the sexiest man she'd ever seen.

"And not a creepy basement?" she blurted.

His grin flashed in the moonlight. "Not a basement. But dark and quiet and talking is frowned upon." He slanted a glance in her direction. "You in?"

Her teeth found her bottom lip, nibbled lightly.

Then she inhaled, exhaled, and thought, *fuck it all*. Maybe it was the booze. Maybe it was Ben and his eyes, his smile, the fantasy of his stubble on her skin.

She met his eyes. "I'm in."

THIS WAS NOT what she'd expected.

Not at all.

She glanced up at the illuminated sign overhead, a vertical set of letters spelling out Cinema, at the white rectangle, black letters spelling out the title of the latest Sci-Fi flick, and felt her heart squeeze tight.

He remembered.

The movie theater was small, only one screen, an old-fashioned box office encased in glass, the smell of popcorn filling the air.

"Still in?" he asked, having returned from the box office with two tickets in hand. He held them up, tiny strips of white paper that were dwarfed by his large hands.

"That depends."

His head tilted to the side, the question written in his eyes.

"Will you let me buy you popcorn?"

His brows drew together. "You want to buy me popcorn?"

Her heart sank. "You don't like popcorn?"

"I love popcorn."

She frowned. "Then what's the problem?"

"You want to buy *me* popcorn?" he repeated.

Ah. She understood where this was going. "You got the tickets. You rescued me. You're driving me around on a whim. The least I can do is get some popcorn." She took his hand, fingers weaving together. There were hard calluses on his palms, and she wondered where he'd gotten them from, what kind of work he did. His profile had just said business owner.

But his hands seemed to scream something physical.

Suddenly, she was imagining him in flannel and a hard hat, or maybe flannel and an ax, all lumbersexual and yummy.

"Come on," she murmured, still filled with that fluffy, fuzzy margarita feeling, although the buzz was fading, and Stef couldn't help but wonder if it was more Ben Buzz and less anything to do with tequila.

"Come on," she said again, tugging him toward the doors. "I'll even spring for candy."

CHAPTER TWELVE

Ben

THERE WAS a giant tub of popcorn between them, two huge sodas settled in the cupholders on opposite armrests.

And candy.

A KitKat and licorice filled with something tart.

More sugar than he'd consumed in years, especially when considering the gallon of soda at his left arm.

But Stef was happily munching away, blasting through the popcorn, and he had to get in there or he might miss the buttery goodness. And then there was the fact that she'd lifted the armrest between them the moment they'd sat down, bringing her lush, gorgeous body close enough for him to smell the floral scent of her, to trace every glorious, curvy line with his eyes, to maybe even touch if he worked up the courage.

"You going to have some?" she asked through a mouthful of popcorn, holding up the bucket.

And fuck, she was cute.

Again.

He took a handful, shoved it in his mouth, and then, not so

casually, slid his arm around her shoulders. She glanced up at him, the flicker of amusement telling him she was well-aware of what he was doing, but she didn't comment, just shifted a little closer, her shoulder tucking under his.

And his cock twitched.

No, not twitched.

It went hard.

And he was wearing fucking sweatpants.

Carefully, he took the bucket and shifted it over to his lap, covering his erection and knowing that he was a fucking pervert when the barest touch of her shoulder to his caused his dick to flare to attention.

"Thief," she accused lightly, but she didn't move or take the popcorn back.

Thank fuck.

Instead, she continued eating and then offered him a piece of KitKat.

He took it, nibbled as she devoured three-quarters of the pack. "You going to puke in my car later?"

Her head tilted against his arm, ponytail a silken sheet on his bare skin. Lips curving, she stared up at him. "I've been told I resemble a Hoover."

"As in the vacuum?"

Her mouth tipped up further. "Exactly."

"And no post-vacuuming puking?"

Her smile didn't fade. "None," she murmured, and then it did. "Ben?" she asked quietly as the lights had gone down.

"Yeah?"

"Thanks for this."

Now, he was the one who was smiling. "You're welcome," he said softly, brushing her hair off her face, tucking a strand behind her ear.

———

SHE'D BEEN RIVETED.

Absolutely riveted by the movie, so focused on the story that *he'd* missed most of it. Because he'd been too absorbed with her. The soft gasps when the tension grew taut, the music building, some plot point blaring to life and making her jump in his arms. The way she cried when one of the main characters died. How she rested against him and sighed in happiness when the space-ship made it back to Earth, most of the crew intact.

Then the credits were rolling, and she was sitting up, and he hated that she'd left him, even though it was just to gather up her trash, even though she was still there, just two feet away. But not in his arms.

Because he liked her there.

"Have you sobered up?" he asked as the lights came back on and they began moving up the aisle.

Her ponytail fluttered behind her as she turned her head to look at him. "Yes." A frown. "Why?"

"If so, I can drive you back to your car," he offered. "That way, you don't have to get a ride in the morning."

Was that a flicker of disappointment over her face?

It was there and gone faster than he could process it, and then she was walking again. "Oh, okay," she whispered, and he barely heard her. But he *did* hear the sad creep into her tone, and yes, the disappointment that had his stomach clenching tight. "That would be great, actually."

One arm held the empty popcorn container, along with her nearly empty cup of soda, his nearly full one, and the candy wrappers.

But he had one arm free.

And *that* was the one he wrapped around Stef's waist, the one he used to draw her back against him, to turn her so every inch of those curves were pressed to him, her breath puffing against his lips.

"What are you doing?" she breathed.

"First date."

Her brows lifted, but she melted against him, and he was hard again, nearly shaking with the need to claim her mouth.

"What is?" she asked. "Do you want to go out—"

"Kiss," he managed, desire making it difficult to form words. But he'd managed that one, and it was a fucking relief.

"Kiss?"

"Yes. Kiss," he said, and through some herculean effort managed to add, "I'm going to kiss you." He slid his hand up, between her shoulder blades, and weaved it into her hair, probably screwing up her ponytail but unable to summon a care. Not when her lips were right there.

Not when she pressed closer.

Not when she took the bucket from him and dropped it to the floor.

"Okay then," she breathed, wrapping her arms around his neck and raising onto tiptoe. "Then kiss me."

Ben lowered his head, slanted his lips across hers, and felt . .
.

Nothing.

Absolutely nothing.

No, not *nothing*. It was . . . peace and coming home and a dark, starlit sky on a summer evening. It was even and steady and balanced—

Stef moaned, her lips parting, her tongue darting out to touch the seam of his mouth.

And the world exploded—or at least *his* did. He was staring straight into the sun and the warmth was washing over him. He'd felt nothing and now he felt *everything*. His nerves were on fire, his dick was granite. She tasted sweet and salty with a floral note beneath. His hands roamed, taking in those curves as she thrust her tongue into his mouth and stroke it against his. The kiss—*she* was fucking glorious, and he was on fire and—

A throat cleared.

Loudly enough that it told him that it wasn't the first time the person had tried to get their attention.

Stef stiffened in his arms, her wide eyes coming to his.

He released her, bent to pick up the bucket, needing it because . . . fucking erections like he was twelve years old. Positioning it in front of him, he turned to face the person who interrupted them. The usher appeared all of eighteen, and though his cheeks were pink, he didn't look at them as he pushed the trash can by them.

"Did you want," Stef asked, her own color high, "to throw—"

Ben shook his head.

"You—"

He glanced down, back up, lifted a brow.

Her cheeks went pinker. "Ah."

Fucking cute.

Fucking not helping his situation.

"Did you want—"

His eyes shot to hers. So help him God, if she tried to get rid of the popcorn container, he was going to use *her* as a shield. Especially since it didn't seem like his erection was going to recede anytime soon.

Not with her swollen lips. Not with her fucking squeezable ass . . . *right there.*

So not helping.

"—to go back to my place?"

His cock surged again, and he almost felt dizzy from the amount of blood gathering in the southern portion of his body. As thus, it took him a moment to gather his thoughts, to be able to speak.

Enough for him to see that disappointment creep into her face.

"Or not—"

He took her hand, drew her against him, rocking his hips

against her ass, knowing it was crude and not giving a shit since it felt so *fucking* good.

"My place is closer," he breathed into her ear.

She shivered, ass tilted back. "Okay then," she murmured.

Then she took his hand and led him from the theater.

CHAPTER THIRTEEN

Stef

HE HELD her hand the entire way back to his condo, one rough finger stroking the inside of her wrist, shivers sliding up her arm, through her middle, and down between her thighs.

She was dripping wet.

She was aching.

Then he parked and opened her door, tugging her up and toward a bank of elevators. A swipe of a card. A code punched into the keypad.

The steel doors opened.

They stepped inside.

And then he was on her.

His body pinning her against one wall, his hands beneath her ass, lifting her so she was propped onto the railing, her legs wrapped around his hips, the fabric between them doing nothing to blunt the hard jut of his cock.

She rocked against it, and he hissed out a breath, the warm puff of air hitting her lips just a heartbeat before he pressed his mouth to hers.

Another kiss, sinking deep into her, pulling her into another dimension where everything felt right and perfect and . . . as though she'd known this man for an eternity. As though she could continue kissing him forever.

The doors opened on an absurd *ping*, and they took a while to pull away from each other, Ben finally drawing back enough to clamp a hand around one of the metal panels when it began to close on them. Grinning, he tugged her off the bar, leading her out of the small metal death box and into the hall . . . or not the hall.

Into an . . . entryway.

Stumbling, she glanced around, brain trying to process mirrors and marble and a large thick white rug that had to be hell to keep clean. "This is your *place?*"

"Yup."

His fingers tight on hers, he drew her down the hall, past a huge kitchen with sleek white cabinets and gray countertops, past a sunken living room filled with a giant TV and a large gray sectional, past a—

Growling filled the air.

"Fuck," Ben hissed, yanking her behind him. "Careful," he said. "I'll grab her and—"

A tiny, fluffy white ball of adorableness sprinted down the hall, her growl far too fierce for her size, the sound of it echoing down all the marble.

He bent, but the pup dodged around him, fur ruffling under his fingers when he released her hand to snag the dog.

"It's okay," she said, kneeling down to meet the little pupper. "Hi, baby." She extended a hand—

"No, *don't.*"

A cold, wet nose grazed the back of hers.

"Stef," Ben ordered. "Stand up, slowly and carefully."

Her eyes found his. "Why—" The dog began licking her hand in earnest before burrowing close, nearly knocking Stef down when she all but crawled into her lap. Sinking back onto her ass, she began scratching and rubbing and found herself being kissed all over.

The last thought had her looking up at Ben, remembering how very close *he'd* been to kissing her all over.

His expression was a mixture of horror and shock.

Maybe he didn't want to kiss a woman all over who'd been on the receiving end of a dog's tongue?

She winced. Yeah, that was probably true.

"I'll . . . uh . . . wash my hands before we . . ." She trailed off, pointed her finger between them. "Continue with—"

Ben blinked and sank down next to her.

The adorable angel in her lap growled.

"She doesn't like me."

Now it was Stef's turn to blink, to wonder why a man who lived in a fucking penthouse with marble and mirrors and a white freaking rug in the entryway was living with a dog who couldn't stand him.

"She doesn't like *anyone*."

Stef blinked again, glanced down at the white floof, trying to reconcile that fact with the sweetheart in her lap. "That's not true," she crooned, lifting her and nuzzling the pup's face. "She's a sweetheart."

"That's her name," Ben said. "But I've never seen her act like one."

"You're Sweetheart?" she asked the pup.

Who responded by kissing Stef's chin.

"Aw, baby," she said, cuddling the dog closer. She was a tiny thing, mostly fur and bones and when Stef stood, holding her against her chest, the pup snuggled against her, and it had to be the cutest thing she had ever seen.

"I'll put her in her crate," Ben murmured, reaching for her.

Sweetheart growled.

"Do we have to?" Steff asked, sending sad eyes in his direction.

His were filled with heat. "We don't," he murmured. "We can hang on the couch and watch *Dr. Pol*."

"I *love Dr. Pol!*" she exclaimed.

He groaned and let his head drop back. "Not you, too."

"I admit I cringe at the surgery parts—"

"I think that's the masochist's *favorite* part," he quipped, nodding toward the pooch. "She's particularly focused when the good doctor starts castrating."

Stef winced. "So, maybe not *Dr. Pol?*"

Big brown eyes on hers. "Whatever you want, baby."

Baby.

It slid down her nape, trailed across her breasts, tightening her nipples, curling in her abdomen, filling the space between her thighs.

She glanced from the pooch to the man.

Though one was cute, the other was responsible for the fact that her pussy was wet. "Where's her crate?" she asked. "I'll put her away."

The grin that Ben gave her had more moisture gathering between her legs, had desire flooding her senses. Her muscles were drawn tight over her skeleton. Her limbs trembled. Her nerves fired, sending sparks across the surface of her skin. Her lips—both sets of them—were tingling.

"This way," he said, leading her down the hall and into one of the bedrooms . . . that had been converted into a doggy play-room. Numerous beds and toys were scattered across a plush rug, a water fountain took up space in one corner, a crate with a pale pink cover in the other.

He held the kennel door wide for her and with a kiss to Sweetheart's head, she tucked the pup inside. Ben locked it in place, ignoring the rumble of displeasure from Sweetheart.

They both stood, and his mouth was still curved.

"You tame wild beasts in addition to Hoovering popcorn?"

Stef laughed as she stepped toward him. "Apparently, I have *two* superpowers."

Then she kissed him.

And found peace and heat, calm and tornado of desire, all at once, all in an instant. Her fingers dug into his shoulders, trying to get closer, even though every inch of her was pressed to every hard inch of him. His tongue didn't hesitate this time, just slid right into her mouth, coaxing hers into a rhythm that was as effortless as breathing.

She clung to him, held on as he transformed her.

Suddenly, she was lifted into his arms again as Ben spun them, pinning her against the wall. Her ankles clasped around his waist, his cock ground into her.

"Fuck," she whispered, her head falling back as his mouth trailed down her throat.

A nip to her collarbone had her bucking against him.

Another had her hands sliding beneath his shirt, feeling the smooth expanse of his skin, blazing hot and threatening to reduce her to ash.

But she walked right into that fire, drawing his mouth back to hers, clenching her legs tighter around him, bucking her hips against his and riding the rigid length of his cock.

So. Fucking. Good.

"Stef," he groaned, tearing his lips from hers again, this time trailing them over to her ear and lightly biting down on the lobe. She shivered and tilted her head to the side, giving him better access, falling into the fucking gloriousness of that hot mouth and silken tongue playing against her skin.

"God, Ben," she moaned. "That's—"

She groaned in protest when he unhitched her legs, set her feet on the floor. His fingers clasped hers, drew her from the room, pulled her farther down the hall to a set of double doors, kicking them open.

"Wow," she breathed.

But then she barely had time to suck in a breath before he was sweeping her back up into his arms, walking across the room. A gasp escaped her when she found herself falling onto a thick mattress, his body coming down onto hers. "This okay?" he asked huskily.

It was fucking perfect.

She didn't tell him that, though.

Instead, she wrapped her arms around him and tugged him down to her, said only, "More."

Another grin that set her insides on fire.

And then he gave her *more.*

CHAPTER FOURTEEN

Ben

MORE.

She wanted more.

She was going to get more, every fucking bit of him.

Dropping *more* of his weight into her, he took her mouth again, tasting that sweet and floral ambrosia on her lips, her tongue. Her nails bit into his scalp, pulling him even closer, until he was between her thighs, only the layers of their clothing between them.

He needed to do something about that.

But he couldn't tear himself away from her mouth, from her taste in order to do so. Her mouth was a drug, her body another. He needed to taste and touch and—

She shoved him back, rolling him over and yanking her shirt over her head.

Pale skin, a plain beige bra. Not lace, not particularly sexy, and yet it was still the best thing he'd ever seen. Her fingers went to the button on her jeans, and he moved, flipping them again and taking over the task, undoing the zipper, yanking them down her legs, chucking one shoe then the another.

They landed behind him with a *thunk*.

His eyes drifted down to her feet, clad in ankle socks that were printed with pink-haloed unicorns.

He grinned. "Unicorns?"

A shrug, her breasts jiggling in that bra, and his mouth watered. "I like fictional critters."

"Hmm." He bent, nibbled on her ankle. "They'll stay on."

She laughed, reached for her underwear. "But hopefully not these." Her fingers slipped beneath the waistband, began nudging them down. Then she paused. "Do you have a condom?" Her fingers slipped out, she turned for the door. "Because I can go get—"

A brush of his lips to hers.

Then he reached into the nightstand, pulled out a box of condoms.

One he'd bought after his message had gone unanswered, part of him hopeful, the other part resentful and thinking he might open that box with someone else. And one that had remained unopened since.

"Oh," she murmured.

"Oh," he agreed.

He was about to order her to get her hands back into her panties when she shifted her hips, pushed down the plain cotton then, just as he was reveling in the flash of cropped brown curls, her back arched and she reached behind her, unclipping her bra and tossing it to the side.

Ben had no fucking clue where it had landed.

He couldn't summon a fuck.

Not when Stef was naked and on his bed. Curves. Red lips. Fuck, he couldn't wait to taste every inch.

So he did—

Or at least, he intended to.

But then she placed a hand on his chest, stopping him. His heart sank, disappointment curling through him, certain she had changed her mind. "Off." She reached for the hem of his shirt, and only then did he relax enough to tear it over his head, to shove his sweats down and remove his shoes.

He kept his boxer briefs on because it would be far too easy, too tempting to slip back between her thighs, to slip *inside* her slick center. Even now, the moisture glistened on her thighs, making his mouth water, his desire the heavy strum of a bass guitar.

Take. Take. Take.

Patience.

"Okay?" he murmured when she abruptly sat up.

"You are the sexiest man I've ever seen," she said, her voice a rasp that slid over his skin, even before her fingers trailed it—caressing over his shoulders, down his arms, up over his abdomen before coming to a rest on his chest. They blazed, the heat sinking into him, scorching down his spine, his cock growing even harder.

His cheeks felt hot at the compliment, but thankfully he didn't have to worry about her seeing it. "You're beautiful." He moved so he was back over her, bracing himself on one hand, using the other to smooth back her hair. "I've dreamed about kissing these lips."

"And getting my lipstick all over you," she said, smiling up at him, her thumb running along his bottom lip. "All because I'm vain."

"Vain?" he asked, smoothing his palm up her side.

Her skin was silk beneath him. "I can't live without my lipstick." A shrug, her ribs moving beneath his palm. "So, yes, vain."

"Should I tell you that I've been dreaming of red lips for months now?"

Her mouth curved. "So, at least vain has a purpose?"

"Yes," he said, leaning down and dragging his mouth along her jaw, pausing at her earlobe. "But only if I get to taste them again."

She smiled and tilted her chin up.

And then there were no more words.

His tongue was in her mouth, his lips on hers then, when his lungs protested, trailing them down, stopping to pay homage to her breasts, suckling and nipping and deducing what she liked best—hard, steady pulls on her nipples. Then he was moving down again, across the soft curve of her belly, allowing his tongue to drift along her hips . . . and still down.

Nudging her thighs apart.

Moving in between.

Kissing up one thigh and skipping the part he was desperate to taste, wanting her writhing beneath him. He might not have had a hundred women, might have been a late bloomer and be uneasy with words, but he paid attention. He knew people, could read them.

Could read *her*.

How her legs trembled when he nipped, how her hands found their way into his hair and tugged when he brought the flat of his tongue up, when he slid it along the outside of her labia, darted it out to taste the sweetly tart folds.

"Fuck," he groaned. That was good.

Her lips parted on a moan, and she drew him closer, her legs wrapping tight, moisture flooding his mouth. Ben didn't stop, just continued to figure out all the things she liked—how much pressure, the way he circled his tongue, how he used the flat of it to press against the bundle of nerves. But when he slid a finger inside her damp tightness, she arched beneath him, and when he slid another in, she bucked, his name tumbling from her tongue.

He sucked her clit deep, curved his fingers, and his name became a chant.

"Ben, Ben, Ben—"

The best sound on the planet.

No.

He was wrong. The best sound on the planet happened next. When her body bowed on the mattress, when she ground her pussy against his mouth, when every muscle in her body was tight, straining.

And then she exploded.

A gasp. A long, trailing moan.

She went limp, her pussy clenching around his fingers.

She was beautiful, her color high, her lips swollen, sweat glimmering on her brow, and then those red lips tugged up into a smile, and she crooked a finger at him. "Come inside me."

He wasn't done. Not nearly.

He'd had months to plan this. Months to think about everything he wanted to do to her.

But when she smiled at him like that, when she crooked her finger, he knew he couldn't deny her anything. Reaching for the box of condoms as he slid up her body, Ben tore open the top and took her mouth at the same time. His hands were busy—one on the bed next to her side to not crush her, one on the box—so he couldn't fend off hers.

Not that he tried very hard, if he was being honest.

Because her hands had slid down his abdomen, slipped beneath the waistband of his underwear, and grasped him tight.

Groaning, he thrust into her hand, into those firm fingers.

"You're hard," she whispered. Though the statement was nonsensical—because *of course* he was hard, he was harder than he'd ever been in his life—the statement sent fire to his cock. He knew it was weeping, that he was seconds away from exploding.

After yanking a condom out of the box, he jerked her hands off him then tore open the packet with his teeth, rolled it down, chucked his underwear to the side, and . . .

Inhaled.

Because he knew that once he was inside that tight, wet heat, he wouldn't be able to stop, wouldn't last long.

So, he clenched his jaw, sucked in one more breath, and then set about turning her into an absolute frenzy of need. He took her mouth, returned to her breasts. Not gently. None of it was gentle. He suckled her breasts, drove his fingers in between her legs, his thumb on her clit, his finger inside.

She gasped and moaned and clung to him, and then he heard the hitch in her breathing again, knew that she was close.

Thank fuck.

He prowled down her body, positioned himself, and . . . glanced up at curves, at red lips, at pretty brown eyes.

Her pupils were huge. Her mouth tempted him.

"Now, Ben." Her smile was almost feral as she moved before he could, gripping his ass with one hand, wrapping a leg around his hip, and finally . . . finally drawing him inside.

They both moaned.

She clenched around him—her leg, her pussy, her arms.

He'd been right.

He wasn't going to be able to last long. But thankfully, she wasn't going to either.

Her hips met his, her fingers clenched on his ass, his shoulder, and they *moved*. A rhythm that was instinctual, that didn't take any effort to stumble into. They were two sides of the same coin, knowing each other without struggle.

And it was good.

And it . . . wasn't going to last long.

He slid a hand up, cupped Stef's breast, running his finger back and forth across the hard bud of her nipple. She clenched tighter, arched further, her head falling back onto the pillow, her lips parted on a moan.

She went over the edge, and not a moment too soon. His orgasm was coiling in the base of his spine, threatening to explode out through his cock.

One stroke.

Another.

He toppled, pleasure dousing him from head to toe, a steaming bucket of water dumped over his head. It soaked into his skin, settled into his very bones, so much fucking bliss washing over him that it took every bit of effort to not collapse on top of her.

But then Stef made a mewl of complaint, tugged him down, and he lowered himself to the mattress, barely summoning the energy to roll to his side and gather her close.

Their breaths came in rapid gusts.

He'd been cracked open, reformed, every past experience erased from his mind until the only thing that remained was Stef—beautiful, intoxicating, Stef.

She nuzzled into his neck, and then she laughed.

"What?" he asked, smoothing a hand down her back.

"That was—" She laughed again. "That was fucking incredible."

Ben froze, his arms tightly around her, his lungs still straining, the sweat not yet dry on his body, and . . . he laughed, too.

CHAPTER FIFTEEN

Stef

EVENTUALLY, Ben slid out of bed to take care of the condom, and Stef knew that she should get dressed, should either take him up on the ride or see if the surge in demand had eased so she could get back to her car.

It was late, they'd gone to the midnight showing, so it must be nearing four. God, she hadn't been up this late in years. Not since her college years—and her all-nighters hadn't ever included great sex. Great *studying* maybe, but not sex. Oh, the sex itself had been good, definitely satisfying. Her partners had always been fun, and she wasn't shy between the sheets. So she had enjoyed herself and especially enjoyed the orgasms that weren't courtesy of her own fingers, but it had never been like this.

Never been this . . . incredible.

She could easily get addicted.

She could easily end up wanting something that would wind up with her brokenhearted.

That happy thought killed her post-orgasm glow, and Stef pushed out of bed. She should go before this got weird. Maybe set up another time for some incredible sex. It was late. She was tired. Plus, Fred would be missing her.

He'd need to go out to the bathroom in a couple of hours, would be wondering where she was.

She didn't leave him, except for doggy day care, and he would worry.

So she searched for her panties, yanked them up her legs, and was just reaching for her bra when Ben walked back into the room.

"What are you doing?" he asked, prowling over to her, his delicious body on display.

"I need to get home," she said. "Fred will be waiting for me."

His brows drew together, the light from the hallway enough that she didn't miss the blast of fury in his eyes. Then they cleared. "Your dog."

"Yup." She pulled on her bra.

He frowned. "Why don't you stay for a couple of hours? Get some sleep, and I'll drive you to your car in the morning."

She yawned. "It *is* morning," she said. "And Fred will be worried."

Something else in his eyes, but he merely nodded then moved around the room, gathering up the remainder of her clothing and handing it to her. Then he went through a door, and flicked on a light, illuminating a closet.

He came back out as she was stepping into her shoes, fully dressed, a hoodie in his hands, thrusting it at her. "It'll be cold."

There went her heart again.

It was dangerous how vulnerable the sliver of kindness made her. The care that he presented was nothing. She'd seen inside his closet, saw the racks of clothes. Surely, he wouldn't miss one sweatshirt.

But it still meant a lot.

Because he'd thought about it.

About her.

"Thanks," she whispered, tugging it over her head and slipping into the bathroom to use the facilities and to wash her hands.

He wasn't in the bedroom when she came out, and she strolled down the hall, popping in to say goodbye to Sweetheart on her way out. The little pup was curled up in the back of her crate, her eyes closed, but she gave Stef a tail wag and lick on her hand when she reached in and scratched Sweetheart between her ears.

"Bye, baby," Stef crooned, locking up and turning off the light in the dog room, her lips twitching when she saw that Ben had rigged up several nightlights that left the space in a comforting glow.

Ben was standing across the hall, so handsome that she felt her heart lurch.

"I can't believe you tamed the beast," he said, his voice roughened velvet that slipped between her legs. Combined with that and the spicy scent of his sweatshirt surrounding her, and she thought she might already be addicted.

One hit and she'd gone down the rabbit hole.

"She's not so bad," Stef said, walking past him. He held her purse, apparently having retrieved it from wherever she'd dropped it.

Maybe the white rug.

Maybe the hall.

Honestly, she couldn't remember.

"Tell that to the dozens of pet sitters and everyone in my office who have either quit or are terrified of her."

Stef took the purse when he held it out. "I'm hoping the quitting is related to the pet sitters and not your employees?"

A grin that sunk like an arrow into her heart.

If an arrow was good.

Okay, that was a horrible analogy, but still she felt the impact of his grin like it was something physical.

"The quitters were the dog sitters," he said, inclining his head to the front door. "The terrified are my employees."

"Poor things."

"When you have a snarling beast chasing you, tell me how you'd react."

Stef snorted. "What is she? All of four pounds?"

"Four-point-*six* frightening pounds."

Laughter bubbled in her chest. "That point-six makes a difference."

"Damn right, it does."

He held the door open—or rather, pushed the button to call the elevator—and after a few moments the panel slid open, the silver doors parting behind it, and they stepped on.

"A private elevator is pretty fancy."

His eyes slid to hers. "Perk of owning the building."

Her brows lifted. "That's fancy, too," she said. "And here I was proud of paying off my Prius."

He went quiet, very quiet, and she almost felt him spooling back into himself, locking down the outer layers and locking them down tightly.

"I'm kidding." She touched his arm. "My friend's mom owns one of the big cosmetics businesses, so I know that money can make some people feel awkward." A wince. "Sorry if my lame attempt at fishing for a joke did the same. She prefers directness, and I shouldn't have assumed you are the same."

Still quiet.

The doors opened and she stepped off, immediately seeing the exit of the underground garage and turning toward it.

Ben caught her arm. "My car's that way."

She shrugged him off. "I know." She moved to the exit.

Suddenly, his broad, hard body was an inch from her nose, and she was reminded how she hadn't had enough time to explore it. She wanted her mouth on every centimeter, wanted to tease out every single sensitive nook and cranny.

"What the fuck are you doing?" he snapped.

"I'm just going to get a Lyft," she said. "You've done more than your due diligence and—"

She yelped in surprise when he suddenly had her pinned against the wall.

He didn't hurt her, quite the opposite, actually. He'd weaved his arms around her, his hands a barrier between the wall and her body. "What the fuck are you doing?" he snapped again.

"I'm going home," she said into those eyes of deep, deep russet. Beautiful eyes. His picture on the app hadn't done them justice. "Go to bed, Ben. You've done more than your fair share tonight."

His brows dragged together.

Sparks flashed in those beautiful eyes.

And then he didn't say anything, just wrapped his fingers around her arm, and said, "I'm driving you home."

Stef knew she could argue, knew she probably should. The need to give in and let him take care of her was certainly the biggest reason for it. The fact that she'd made him uncomfortable in the elevator was another. Her addiction, still one more. But . . . she just wanted a little more time.

Because, who knew if she'd see him again?

Because she'd been groomed over and over again to expect that any good times would invariably come to an end.

So probably, she should retreat, protect herself.

Instead, she did what she always did. The stupid, idiotic thing. She reached out and grasped on.

"Okay," she said.

She'd barely gotten the agreement out before he was guiding her over to the car. Her purse slipped down her arm, and he snagged it for her, opening her door and waiting for her to sit down before buckling her in. The metal panel shut, and he walked around the car, opening his own door and dropping into his seat. Gently, he set the purse down at her feet, started up the engine, and backed out of the stall.

Through the city streets . . . in silence.

To the freeway . . . in silence.

South toward her house . . . in silence.

She thought of a dozen things to say and just as quickly dismissed them. Too tired. Too vulnerable. Too—

His hand rested on her knee, and she jumped, jarred out of her thoughts.

Immediately, he withdrew, and she opened her mouth to tell him that she hadn't jumped because of him, had rather just been so locked into her thoughts that she'd forgotten she wasn't alone.

For God's sake! Get out of your head, Stef.

And while it was always a shitty time to hear Jeremy's voice, it was especially a shitty time when it was—her eyes flicked to the dash to see the time—4:36 in the morning.

God, she could fuck the man, but she couldn't talk to him?

Say something. *Anything.*

Thanks for the orgasms and the movie, let's do it again.

You're sexy and I want to give you my number.

Please, don't ghost me like I ghosted you.

Thank you for the ride and the—

But the words stayed locked on her tongue, in her mind, in her throat, and then she looked out the window and realized where she was.

Nearly at her condo.

Well, she supposed with a yawn, that she'd just get her car after she slept. She was probably too tired to drive anyway.

"What number?" Ben asked, both hands now clenched tight on the steering wheel. Strong hands, strong fingers, fingers that had been inside her.

His eyes came to hers, and she blinked. "On the end. White mailbox."

He nodded, navigated to her driveway and pulled the car to a stop.

Her throat was still tight, the words still stoppered up. "Thanks," she managed to squeeze out. "For the—"

Ben opened his door and got out so quickly that she was still talking when the door shut, still blinking at his movements when hers opened. He reached in, unbuckled her seat belt, and snagged her purse, waiting for her to get out before trailing her to the door.

She unlocked the door, stepped inside.

Ben waited on the porch, and she was summoning more words when Fred came bounding down the hall, a soft "woof" in the air that had her ordering, "Wait."

Her good boy waited.

Her . . . complicated, confusing man *also* waited.

Although Ben wasn't hers.

They'd watched a movie. They'd fucked. They'd talked a bit. He wasn't *her* anything.

Fred crept forward, his feet not crossing that invisible barrier of the threshold, even though his nose crept over it, smelling Ben's hand when he held it out. Tentatively. Fred sniffed and then licked and then, as per his usual, his tail went propellor.

"Wait," she reminded him.

He plunked his butt on the floor and looked up adoringly at Ben, who carefully and slowly set her purse on the porch before bringing his other hand down and beginning to scratch the sides of Fred's head, his ears, his neck.

Fred practically turned into a puddle.

"You're a good boy, aren't you, buddy?" Ben murmured, and his rough, sexy voice had *her* melting into a puddle, desperate for him to call her a good *girl*.

"Thank you," she blurted.

Ben had crouched as he scratched Fred, and now he glanced up at her, those eyes deep, unreadable pools of brown.

He still didn't say anything.

"And I'm sorry about the elevator and that you had to drive out to pick me up—"

"I'm not."

But the words that had been smothered in her voice box

were now out in full force, a different kind of smothering, a blurt that filled the air with unnecessary words. "And I know it was an inconvenience for you to come get me and to bring me home and probably the movie, too, since you hadn't planned on going out. And then I made it weird in the elevator, and I like your rug in the entryway, but how doesn't it get dirty? And—"

He cupped her cheek. "Goodnight, Stef." He brushed his lips over hers, released her. And as she was still catching her breath, he bent again, snagged her purse, and put it over the threshold, then reached for the handle.

The door *snicked* closed.

She stared at that closed panel of wood and knew that she'd had her fun.

And now it would be done.

"Goodbye, Ben," she whispered.

———

IN THE MORNING—OR rather, well in the *afternoon*—Stef managed to peel herself out of bed and shower.

Her body was deliciously sore, long unused muscles tense from their exertions.

But the shower went a long way to making her human, along with a bagel absolutely slathered with her cinnamon cream cheese. And coffee. Couldn't forget regenerating herself with the hearty, black brew.

By the time she was human again, she retrieved her purse and her phone and started to call up the app to get a ride to the restaurant.

Then she happened to walk by her family room.

Or rather, by the large window in the family room, her gaze catching on . . . her car in the driveway. That couldn't be.

Mouth falling open, she lurched for the door and yanked it open.

A blue Prius. The right passenger's side rim a little damaged since she sucked at parallel parking. A golden retriever shaped air freshener hanging from the rearview. She couldn't check the license plate, because she never remembered the combination of numbers and letters—though she *could* recall it having a seven, which this Prius also had.

Except . . . she'd left her car at the bar.

Frowning, she moved closer to it, glancing inside to see the collection of trash on the floor (since she was one of those messy car people), along with several empty disposable coffee cups crammed into the cupholders.

Her cell buzzed in her hand, and she stared down at it in confusion.

Part because it was a text message, and one that appeared to be from Ben.

Part because her car had mysteriously appeared in her driveway.

The text only said.

Mailbox.

Another blink.

More confusion.

But she made her way to her mailbox, tugged open the little door, and saw the envelope inside. "Um, okay," she muttered, snagging it and tearing open the top, even though she'd already suspected and could feel what was inside.

Her car keys.

She blipped the locks, just to make sure, and predictably, the lights flashed, the locks clicking open.

Her heart seized, squeezing hard enough to take her breath away.

How he'd done it, she didn't know. Well, she supposed she knew how he'd done it, snagging her keys from her purse at some point—her car fob was separate from her set for the house, since she had all of her work keys on that same ring and hated the noise of them rattling when they hung from the ignition.

Still, she didn't know *how*.

Or maybe the more important question was that she didn't know *why*.

She'd gone to bed thinking she would never hear from him again, thinking that all his quiet meant that he was done with her.

And then he'd fetched her car.

Or had someone do it for him, considering he owned that penthouse with the private elevator—considering he owned that entire building. San Francisco real estate prices were insane. That told her enough about his financial status. The man probably had underlings for days.

Retrieving a car was nothing more than a nice man doing a nice thing.

And washing his hands of her.

She frowned.

Hating that thought.

Hating that it chased her all the way inside.

CHAPTER SIXTEEN

Ben

HE DIDN'T TURN on his car until after Stef went inside, even though exhaustion was pulling at his eyelids.

He'd kept up his vigil from the moment he'd dropped Stef off. Staying until it was a semi-reasonable hour and he'd called Baine and Spence to come and retrieve the keys. Waiting as they'd gone and returned with the car, parking it in Stef's driveway. Baine had come to Ben's window after stashing the keys in the mailbox as ordered, grinning like a lunatic and asking, "Anything you want to tell me?"

"F.I.R.E.D," he'd responded.

To which Baine had just grinned and shaken his head. "Car needs a wash."

Maybe he'd arrange that next.

"Go home," he said. "And take Monday off. I know it's not your favorite waking up at dawn to work on a Saturday."

Baine stared at him, shook his head, and started walking over to Spence's car. "I'll see you Monday," he called over his shoulder.

"Baine—"

His assistant spun back. "I didn't do it because you're my boss," he said, closing the distance between them. "Spence did," he added with a jerk of his chin, "because he hasn't been around long enough to know that you fucking bend over backward for us every chance you get."

Ben sucked in a breath.

"You know how many times you've ever asked me for a favor?" Baine demanded. "On a Saturday or otherwise?"

Ben shook his head.

"Never." Baine's jaw clenched and then relaxed. "You've done me a shit-ton of them, starting with giving me the job even though my dumbass lied on the application, letting me have time off to be with my daughter anytime I needed it, giving me raises I didn't deserve when her mom disappeared—"

"You deserved them."

Baine just continued talking. "I didn't," he said, "I was barely around for those six months, and then when I finally got my shit together and was able to focus on work, when Beth"—his baby mama—"showed back up, fucked up out of her mind, you hooked me up with that lawyer. She helped me get full custody, even though I knew that it wasn't an easy fight. Who helped me get her into that good preschool? Who set me up with the nanny?"

Ben's hands clenched into fists, the words rolling over him.

It was nothing.

All of that was hardly anything.

"You're a good dad," he told Baine, "and Lei deserves to have you in her life all the time. She deserves a good school and you work better for me if you know she's secure."

Baine tapped the frame of the car. "I know," he said. "She deserves the fucking world." His pale blue eyes locked on Ben's. "And you gave it to her. So, don't you ever act like you asking me for one thing outside of work is an inconvenience.

You haven't been just my boss for years. You're my friend, and I have your back."

Ben sucked in a breath, wanting to disagree, to tell him not to bother.

But Baine probably recognized that opposition rolling up his throat, dancing on the tip of his tongue. "See you Monday," he said.

"Spence—"

"Will be there, too."

"Fuck," Ben muttered, rolling up his window and preparing to drive away. He needed to get home, needed to see what kind of trouble Sweetheart had gotten into. Claire—another favor he owed—had let her out of the kennel earlier that morning, had fed her.

And though she'd texted and said that Sweetheart had been markedly . . . sweet—or at least sweet for her (meaning she hadn't attempted to bite ankles, instead just grumbling her way to her food dish), he knew he couldn't ignore his responsibilities. Even if he was tempted to walk right up to Stef's door and take credit for returning her car.

And take something else.

"Fuck," he muttered again, hitting the ignition and reaching for the gear shift.

His phone buzzed.

He started to ignore it, thinking that Baine was going to give him more shit, but when his eyes caught on the contact's name, his heart thudded. Once and very hard against his ribs.

Red Lips.

Stef.

His cock went hard.

How'd you get my number?

His fingers were typing before he fully processed picking up his cell.

I have my ways.

A beat then,

Like the ways you managed to get my car mysteriously back in my driveway?

His lips twitched.

Yep.

Another buzz.

I thought you'd forgotten. I was just going to get it today.

He replied.

I know. But you were tired, and it wasn't any trouble.

Not for him, anyway. Baine, who'd had to call in his nanny, and Spence, who'd had to get his and Baine's asses to the restaurant at the butt crack of the morning, they might say differently.

Even though they specifically *hadn't* said differently.

Even though he was ignoring that part.

A heartbeat passed.

I keep having to thank you.

He sent back,

You don't, you know.

The "…" appeared. Then,

I do. But not because I feel obligated. Because I am thankful. Those were really kind things you did and—

Ben waited for her to finish the rest of the text. When she didn't, he typed out a reply.

And what?

Long moments passed.

And I just wanted to say thank you because that was kind, even though I know I made things weird. That's my super-power, making things weird.

He smiled.

I thought your superpowers were Hoovering and taming beasts.

Only a couple of seconds before she replied.

You've discovered my evil secret. I, in fact, have three superpowers.

Ben chuckled.

I'm a lucky, lucky man.

He pressed send, and a full minute passed before she replied.

Will you tell me something?

Anything.

That was what he wanted to send. Instead he typed out something else.

Does it involve my superpowers?

She did that react thing with the message, a little "ha-ha" icon appearing by his text before the "…" went again.

I didn't think I'd hear from you again.

His heart thudded.

He clenched his jaw, forced it to relax. For a moment, in the elevator, he'd thought the same. Thought it would be smarter to let her go. It was never a good sign for someone to talk about his money. He'd been convinced in a couple of sentences that she'd fooled him, that she was after something, after a meal ticket or maybe a funny story to sell the tabloids—*Billionaire has Viscous Dog. Hunt CEO is Too Good to Ride with the Common Folk.*

But then she'd started babbling, explaining about her friend's mom and apologizing, and even then he'd still thought it was a line, a way of trying to get back on his good side, so she could get that meal ticket.

Until she'd headed for the exit.

Until she'd been shocked he had stopped her.

Until he remembered the look on her face when he'd pulled up outside the bar, when he'd offered to drive her to her car, when he'd passed her the sweatshirt.

As though she'd been lacking in receiving kindness.

And the urge to give it to her was instinctual.

He couldn't let her go.

He'd seen her phone flashing inside her purse as he'd tucked her into her seat, had noticed it didn't have a passcode (something he was going to talk to her about soon), and hadn't been able to stop himself from programming in his number, from using it to call his cell so he had hers.

Then as he'd driven, listening to her yawn, her half-lidded stare out the windshield, he'd ignored his previous promise of picking up her car.

He'd programmed her street into his GPS without the number, not wanting to disturb her thoughts, to jar her out of her sleepy state, at least until he'd gotten as far as he was able. Then he'd touched her.

And she'd jumped.

He hated that jump, despised that reaction. He wanted her to be comfortable with him. But he wasn't good with people, at least not outside of the business world. He didn't do soft words, for one, sucked at explanations for his defensive behaviors, for another. So, he was struggling to come up with a way to put her at ease, to let her know that the thing in the elevator wasn't a big deal after all when he'd pulled into the driveway.

Then had still wrestled with it as he'd walked her up to her house.

Had actually considered taking the coward's way out and letting her go in that instant.

Until Fred.

Fucking cute ass dog, and well-behaved, and sweet, and nothing like Sweetheart and all her snarling. He'd actually listened. Then had relaxed into Ben's scratching.

So he'd swooped back into Stef's purse, knowing he was an asshole for invading her privacy like that a second time. But he'd convinced himself it was for a good cause, so he'd swiped the key fob.

He'd retrieved her car.

He wanted to hold on to Stef.

Ben?

Muttering a curse, he yanked himself out of his brain and typed.

That wasn't a question.

A beat.

Oh.

His fingers worked on the screen.

For the record, that wasn't either.

He could almost picture her nibbling at her bottom lip.

Can I take you to dinner? As a thanks?

That had him straightening in surprise. She wanted to take him to dinner. As a thanks? After the orgasm she'd given him?

His shock had him taking too long to reply because his cell vibrated again.

Never mind. That's okay. Thanks again. Have a nice life.

Have a nice life.

The words ricocheted through his insides, startling him into motion, his fingers flying on the screen . . . but not to text Stef.

Instead, they pulled up Claire's contact and hit call.

"I've got the beast," Claire said. "I took her back to my place, and for some reason, she didn't even try to bite me in the process."

Not for some reason.

But for the sunshine inside that house, blasting through the darkness they'd both lived with for too long.

"Gonna tell me why that is?" she pressed.

"No."

A chuckle. "Figured it was worth an ask."

He snorted.

"Figured you'd respond like that, too." A beat. "Which is why I'm telling you, as your new VP, to go . . . play."

Then she hung up, the pain in his ass.

But he didn't ignore her order.

Instead, he got out of his car, walked up the driveway, and knocked on the front door.

CHAPTER SEVENTEEN

Stef

SHE WAS GATHERING her stuff for the beach, intending to make it a longer outing than usual to make up to Fred for her absence the previous night, when there was a knock on the door.

Freezing, remembering what the last knock had brought her to her doorstep, she sucked in a shoring breath and hoped like hell who was on the other side would go away.

The knock came again.

"Fuck," she muttered, rotating from the small wall unit in the entryway where she kept all of Fred's various accoutrements, she leaned to the side and peered through the small window on the side of the door.

Like she probably *shouldn't* have done in that moment.

Because Ben must have seen the flicker of movement, and his deep brown eyes came down onto hers, and heat boiled in her belly.

He didn't knock again, just waited and watched as . . . she flicked open the lock.

He turned the handle, slowly pushed the door back so she had enough time to get out of the way, and she did, stumbling back a step as the panel swung wide, landing with a soft *smack* against the doorstop.

"Going somewhere?"

Fred skidded around the corner, crashing into the wall and running toward them—or rather, toward their new visitor. Stef opened her mouth—

"Wait."

It hadn't come from her. Instead, it slid through the air on Ben's soft but firm baritone, the same voice that had ordered her to "Come" at some point hours before.

She shivered.

Fred plunked his ass on the floor.

They both looked at Ben.

"Going somewhere?" he asked, bending to scratch Fred, whose tail immediately began dusting the floor.

"The beach," she breathed.

He glanced from the bag on her shoulder to Fred. Then back to her.

She shivered again.

"Okay if I come in?"

Was it?

He hadn't replied to her asking him for dinner. Maybe he'd been driving and couldn't? But then he'd been texting fast and furious before, so perhaps he'd . . . gotten a ride with whoever picked up her car, so hadn't seen it?

Or maybe she wouldn't have any of these answers unless she let him in.

Nodding, Stef stepped back, turning and catching the bag on the corner of the door, nearly sending it toppling off her shoulder.

Warm fingers caught it, slid it down her arm.

Another shiver.

And she was bustled backward, the door closing, Ben taking the bag and setting it on the ground before he snagged a hoodie off the hook and thrust it at her. Then when she just stared blankly at it, he stepped behind her, tucked it over her shoulders, and moved her limp arms into the sleeves.

"Better?" he asked, when he'd zipped it for her.

No.

Because now she was both burning up with desire and at risk of plunking her ass on the floor like Fred and begging Ben to deliver some of his touches that had made her melt only hours before.

He touched her cheek. "You want to buy me dinner?"

Her heart squeezed. "Seemed like a fair trade."

"You want to see me again?"

Stef lifted her chin. "You tell me. You're the one who got all quiet last night."

"I tend to . . ." He shook his head. "I'm not great with people outside of a business setting. I can make a deal and charm and schmooze, but talking to a beautiful, smart, funny woman is . . . less comfortable."

Brows lifting, she blurted, "You think it's hard to talk to *me?*"

A small smile. "I'm not exactly a Lothario."

"But . . . you're the sexiest man I've ever seen and—"

His jaw fell open and then he started laughing, bending over at the waist, laughing and shaking his head, and when he glanced back up at her, his lips were curved into a grin that had her heart thumping. "That's the second time you've said that, and now I know you need to get your eyes checked, baby."

Clearly, *he* was the one who needed an optometrist, but she liked his smile so much that she didn't point that out.

And anyway, she knew something of what it was like to look in the mirror and judge oneself. That was part of being a normal human with insecurities, and just because she thought he was beautiful didn't mean that he saw the same in himself. Hell, she'd argue that the dent in confidence was something most people—including her—had.

Funnily enough, that unstuck her enough to cup his cheeks, to step closer.

Too close for hardly knowing him.

Not nearly close enough after the intimacy of last night.

"Thank you for getting me my car."

His eyes flared, one hand covered hers. "You're welcome."

Thud-thud went her heart.

"Dinner?" she asked.

He hesitated, just for the barest moment before he nodded.

Her heart did a happy dance.

"Unless you'd rather come to the beach with us first?"

Another nod, the corners of his mouth turning up.

Not a happy dance this time. No, her heart was cracked open, laid bare, exposed and vulnerable . . . and she fell for him, just a little bit, right then and there.

———

"YOU DO THIS EVERY SATURDAY?" Ben asked, his hands in his pockets, his bare feet mixing with the sand below.

They'd both left their shoes and socks in the car—or in her case, her flip-flops—because she'd gotten one of the primo spots right near the steps that led down to the beach and had backed in.

Fred hadn't even needed the leash she'd now clipped around her shoulders.

She'd just opened the back door, undid his seat belt, and he'd hit the waves.

Even as she'd winced, knowing how cold the ocean was in this part of California.

Not the warm waves of SoCal.

But the biting surf of the Bay Area. Good for swimming only on the rare days it was above ninety here on the coast, when the cold was actually a relief from the blazing heat that reflected off the sand.

She nodded, shifted carefully over a piece of seaweed and felt her ankle clench. "Every Saturday," she agreed. "If only for a short walk. Fred loves the ocean."

Ben turned to stare down at her. "You love it, too."

Stef found her lips curving when Fred turned and barked at a wave that had dared sneak up on him, dousing his tail. "I like to see him like this." She nodded in his direction. "But yes, I like it here, too. Even if it isn't a warm Caribbean beach with clear blue waters, even if there are Great Whites prowling just off the coast, I do love to watch the sun set over waves."

He turned, and she followed his gaze.

The sun was a while away from setting.

"Usually, we go later in the day," she told him, just as Fred came back with a stick and dropped it at her feet. She launched it out into the surf, and he took off for it as she grinned up at Ben. "Otherwise my arm gives out."

Laughter in his eyes as they both watched Fred retrieve the stick and then return it.

She threw.

He ran.

They repeated the pattern until he got distracted by a seagull and dropped it at Ben's feet.

"Oh, you don't have—"

Ben launched the stick much more effortlessly than she had.

And further.

"Is that too far?" he asked, shooting a concerned look in her direction.

She shook her head. "He'd swim forever," she said. "But I usually just make sure to not throw it much farther than the first break."

A quiet gaze studying the surf.

Then he nodded.

"Do you want to sit?"

His eyes came to hers. "Do you?"

She nodded, shifted her weight, and his stare flicked down, that careful, quiet studying now coming to her, to her ankle.

"What happened?" he asked, sitting down.

Following suit, she arranged her legs in front of her, knowing the scar from the surgery was easily spotted, bright pink against the white of her skin. "You didn't notice it last night."

"I didn't say that."

Her eyes darted to his.

"I . . . was more focused on other things."

A bolt of heat slid through her. Indeed, he had been. "Surgery," she offered when that now intense stare, probably remembering what she did—the heat, the pleasure, the *fun*—met hers. They were at a beach with her dog, and she wanted to strip him naked. That, too, was probably obviously displayed in her eyes. "Fred is a good boy"—he dropped the stick; Ben threw it again—"but his fatal flaw is squirrels. The turkey is obsessed with them, and it's the only thing he'll pull at, albeit rarely. I was on call for the lab, and my phone buzzed. I answered it, thinking it was work, when really it was my ex—"

He winced.

She nodded, wondering why she was telling him this part when she hadn't told anyone else about Jeremy calling, about him yelling at her and distracting her, and . . . no, about her stupid self picking up the phone, *allowing* herself to be distracted.

"Fred saw the squirrel. Fred decided that this was his one opportunity out of ten to lunge for the squirrel that had come into his orbit—"

Another wince.

"Yup," she said. "The leash wrapped around my legs and took me down. I fell awkwardly, dropped my purse, my cell, and landed wrong. *Really* wrong. And I remember just lying there, trying to summon the strength to push myself up, to reach for my phone that was just out of reach." She sighed.

"And when I grabbed it, I could still hear my ex being an asshole, yelling about *me* yelling into the speaker when I'd fallen and then continuing on with some grievance about a sweatshirt."

"A sweatshirt."

"I may or may not have decided to keep his comfy sweatshirt after that," she admitted, not really feeling guilty about it, even though she probably should, considering it was stealing. "Because he was a total dick about it, and then I had to have the surgery so it wasn't exactly at the top of my priority list. The worst part is that he didn't even ask if I was okay when I told him I thought I'd broken my ankle." She wrinkled her nose. "He just told me that I'd better drop it by his place and . . ."

She trailed off at the expression on Ben's face.

Thunderous was the mildest description she could come up with.

"He didn't ask if you were okay?"

A deadly question.

"I—"

"You told him you thought you'd broken your ankle, that you'd fallen, and he was worried about a fucking sweatshirt?"

Stef winced. "Um. Yes?"

The only sounds were those of the waves breaking against the shore.

Then Ben asked, "What's his name?"

Now, he looked downright scary, and she knew it must be the ruthless business side of him coming out, the part that made it possible for him to own that building in the city, to make whatever deals were necessary in order to achieve his ends.

Heat curled between her thighs.

Probably, it shouldn't. But the fury had her shifting on the sand, clenching her legs together, wondering what it might be like to unleash that ferocity in bed.

"Stef."

A slightly sharp command, not fierce enough to make her

bristle, but enough to make her wet, to make her want to argue with him, just to see where it would get her.

What was *wrong* with her?

But nearly the same moment, a thought grasped onto the coattails of the first, one that was opposite and important and—

Because what was finally going *right* with her?

She felt blazingly alive. She wanted things, and yeah, so maybe wanting Ben wasn't the same as wanting *things,* as in plural. Though she supposed it was plural in the sense that she wanted to do multiple things *with* him.

"It doesn't matter," she said. "*He* doesn't matter. We've been broken up for almost a year now. My ankle was . . . *God* . . . six? Seven? No, it must have been nine months ago. He's ancient history." A shrug, deliberately ignoring the fact that it hadn't been *that* long since he'd showed up on her porch demanding that stupid vase. She hadn't heard from him since; that was all that mattered. "I've moved on."

"It still hurts you."

Stef shrugged. "It was a bad break. It probably always will ache a bit."

His palm came to her cheek. "And he yelled at you about a fucking sweatshirt instead of helping you."

That was what people did.

People who weren't Ben with his picking up at bars, his returning of cars. He was an anomaly. People weren't good, not like him. Unless you really meant something to them, they didn't go out of their way for others.

And she'd never fallen into the category of meaning enough.

She *wanted* that.

She'd seen what her friends had with their significant others. She'd even been lucky enough to feel the care they gave her as friends. So, she wasn't so cynical as to think that it didn't exist, that she was ultimately unworthy of it.

Stef was a good person. She had some great qualities.

But she was realistic enough to understand that if it came

down to it, her friends would choose their spouses, choose each other. She was the newest addition. Well, Tammy had come after, but she was Kate's sister-in-law, Brad and Jaime's sister. Stef was aware of where she'd fall on the hierarchy.

And look, she knew how that sounded.

Like she'd signed up for a pity party for one.

She hadn't.

She worked in numbers and formulas, within the rules of science. Cause and effect, correlations, associations . . .

They all pointed to the same thing.

She just didn't matter that much to the people in her life, wouldn't matter enough for them to choose her if the world were ending and they could only cling to one person.

Which was morose and dramatic and . . . fine.

Ben's fingers flexed on her cheek, and she forced a smile. "I was fine."

Something flashed through his eyes, telling her he knew that she wasn't going to tell him Jeremy's name—even if it was tempting to allow Ben to unleash whatever businessman badassness he possessed on her ex.

She didn't want to go backward.

She wanted to hold on to this feeling, to enjoy her time with Ben, for however long it lasted.

His thumb brushed over her cheek. "Stubborn."

"Now you know one of my many faults, right along with my superpowers."

"I don't consider being stubborn a fault."

"Liar."

His lips twitched. "Okay, maybe in this instance, I would like you to be a little *less* stubborn, but I know when I've been beaten."

She jumped when a cold, wet nose nudged against her foot.

Ben barely spared a glance, scooping up the stick and launching it away, Fred chasing after it.

His thumb continued stroking, his palm shifting, dragging

down her throat, making her shiver. "Will he really play fetch all night?"

Her lips curved. "Until he passes out on the sand." She lifted and dropped her arm. "Until my arm gives out."

"So, if I kept throwing the"—Fred dumped the stick on Ben's lap, right on cue—"stick," he said, scooping it up and tossing it again. "If I save your arm . . . then what will you give me?"

His hand drifted down beneath the neckline of her sweatshirt, traced across her collarbone. Another quiver, goose bumps rising on her skin.

She shifted closer, her thigh pressing to his, her hand lifting to rest on his chest.

"I'll give you—"

The stick landed on her shins and . . . Fred decided to shake, splashing them both with icy cold ocean water.

She shrieked. *"Fred!"*

Ben froze.

She expected him to curse, to back away, or jerk up to his feet, wiping away the water and glaring at her. It's what Jeremy would have done, if she'd twisted his arm and somehow had managed to get him out here at all. But Ben didn't do that, didn't move at all actually, as water dripped down his cheek.

Stef reached up and wiped the drops away.

The touch had him shifting closer, his words brushing hers on a hot rush of air. "You'll give me . . . what?"

It took her a minute to focus, to remember what she'd been saying before the dousing.

Then she *did* remember.

Her hand slid down his cheek, cupping his jaw, feeling the bristles there against her palm. "A kiss," she murmured. "I'll give you a—"

"Thank fuck," he muttered.

His mouth slammed down onto hers.

CHAPTER EIGHTEEN

Ben

THE DOG WAS TRYING to kill him.

He'd just slanted his lips across hers, and Fred was back, wanting to fetch, and Ben swore to fuck that he'd *just* thrown the damned stick.

He launched it again, a little farther this time, hoping it wasn't too far.

Then Stef's tongue touched the seam of his lips, and he stopped worrying about the dog and started worrying about whether or not he'd be able to stop himself from stripping her naked on the beach and fucking her right there.

Not only would that be uncomfortable—sand, so much sand in all the wrong places—but he didn't want to get either of them arrested.

Plus, naked sand fucking in the middle of the day would certainly hit the gossip sheets.

And he didn't want his bare ass on any blog.

Just as that thought trickled through his mind, Fred dropped the stick on his lap and shook again, and Stef tore her lips away, shrieking again.

"Come on, Fred!" she snapped.

Her pooch just nudged the stick closer and wagged his tail.

Ben captured a drop of water where it trailed down her throat, scooping it up with his thumb, and she shivered again. Though he was finally getting it through his thick skull that it was less from cold and more from him.

Which he was just enough of a posturing alpha to appreciate.

Especially when she leaned close and buried her face in his throat, her lips grazing his skin, her soft exclamation of "Kryptonite" reaching his ears.

Ben laughed. "I was thinking the same thing." A beat. "Well, that and along with needing a third person to chuck the stick so I could kiss you properly." She giggled, and he found his fingers in her hair again, the soft locks dancing along the back of his hand. "You okay?"

She nodded. "Though I could do without another Fred dousing."

Speaking of which, the pooch came back with the stick and Ben scooped it up, throwing it before he had the chance to stop and shake.

"Smart man," Stef teased.

He laughed. "I occasionally can be," he said, slipping his hand from her hair and wrapping it around her shoulders when she wiggled closer. "But usually, I just get lucky."

"What do you do, anyway?"

This was the part that always got dicey and uncomfortable and . . . people just got weird when they found out that he ran Hunt Inc. It was too big, too often in the news, too strange knowing he was the brains of the giant conglomeration, that it —and he—was worth that much.

She sensed his hesitation. "Never mind," she told him. "You don't have to tell me if it makes things awkward."

Except, it was one of the most innocuous questions she could ask him, wasn't it?

It was also an important one.

Something he needed to share if he wanted to have her in his life. Because that was what this came down to, wasn't it? She'd sent that text, giving him the way out, and he had known in an instant he hadn't wanted that. He wanted her, *had* wanted her from the moment he'd spied those red lips, from the short conversation, hadn't been able to stop thinking about her, in all honesty.

He hadn't even stopped to think when she'd said she couldn't get a ride.

He'd just known it had to be him.

Same as the movies, the food, those moments with Sweetheart . . . the sex. The *car*.

Him. Him. *Him.*

"I work at the lab"—she named one of the big biotech firms in the area—"with my friend, Heidi. Well, really, she's my boss, but she kind of bullied me into being her friend when she realized that I was alone here and things with Jeremy—"

He stiffened.

She glanced up at him, her eyes going wide. Then they narrowed. "Forget you heard that."

Not a chance in hell.

But he didn't comment as her coffee-colored eyes remained on his, continued *glaring* at him.

"You're not going to forget that, are you?"

He just lifted his brows.

"You're not," she muttered. "Well, anyway, Heidi took me under her wing, and then it wasn't just Fred and me any longer. We had Kate, Cora, and Kelsey—they'd all been friends since college. We also got Tammy, who's Kate's sister-in-law who moved to town not long ago. And Kels's fiancé, Tanner, Kate's husband, Jaime, and Heidi's husband, Brad. Brad and Jaime are brothers and Tammy is their sister, and they're just all really nice people. Kate's mom, Marabelle, is the one who owns the cosmetics company . . ."

Ben could admit this was the point that he began tuning out, just began watching those lush lips move, throwing the stick when Fred came back, and wondering how long it would be until he could kiss her again.

Stef realized that. Or at least she realized that she'd lost him in the sea of names. Probably, she wasn't all that aware of the need burning through him, not his shirt conveniently placed over one bent leg.

Sweats would be dangerous around this one.

"Sorry," she said, so softly he could barely hear her over the crash of the waves. "That was a lot to throw at you."

He tugged her a little closer, smothering a groan when her palm brushed his thigh. "I'm probably not going to remember all of those names," he admitted, "but I like hearing you talk."

Her brows shot up. "You like . . . hearing *me*"—her voice squeaked here—"talk?"

Ben couldn't resist brushing a kiss over her forehead. "Yes."

"Just to clarify," she said. "Me?"

Laughter bubbled up in his chest, burst out of him. So fucking cute. "Yes," he said again, bopping her lightly on the nose. "Squeak aside, you have a pleasant voice, and I'm glad your boss bullied you into friendship."

Stef's eyes went wide, concern drifting into those coffee-colored depths. "I was kidding about the bullying part. She's not like that."

"I know."

A slow blink. "*How* do you know?"

"Because of the way your face looks when you talk about her, about them."

Another blink, surprise weaving its way through her expression. "What do I look like?"

"Your face gentles and light comes into your eyes."

"Oh."

It was a whisper, her gaze going out to the horizon and no stranger to needing a few quiet moments, he let her have this one. Just picked up the stick and threw it several more times, his stare alternating from the setting sun, to Stef, to Fred.

"I love them," she said, turning back toward him when the sun had turned into a half circle, the rest of it slipping beyond the skyline. "I didn't realize how much I did until you said that." She glanced at him, then away again, her voice nearly inaudible. "I didn't realize how much I'm going miss them when it's over."

He straightened. "Why would it be over?"

Was she moving? Fuck, was she *dying*?

His mind immediately went worst-case scenario, picturing his mom wasting away, the cancer taking her piece by piece.

She just shook her head, not looking at him.

"Stef?" he asked. "Are you sick?"

Something in his tone—probably the panic—had her glancing back. "No," she said. "I'm fine. My friends are fine."

"Are you moving?"

"No."

Then what the fuck are you talking about? he wanted to yell.

But there was something fragile about her in that moment, something even Fred, as though sensing her disquiet, seemed to recognize, sprawling on the sand next to her, the stick forgotten, his side pressed to her leg. She didn't protest against Fred's wet fur soaking through her jeans, just stroked her fingers through it and silently watched the sun go down.

So, he did the same.

Even though he had a million questions running through his mind.

CHAPTER NINETEEN

Stef

BEN TOOK the towel from her hands, efficiently rubbing the worst of the sand and water from Fred's fur.

She knew it wouldn't all get out.

Sundays were Fred's bath day.

He lifted Fred into the car, buckled his seat belt, leaving her to stand uselessly to the side of the car, watching the strong lines of his body do something that was often a struggle for her.

Fred, as previously established, was a good boy. He, however, wasn't graceful while navigating hallways or chasing squirrels or jumping into cars. Most of the time he jumped and missed, crashing his face into the seat, so mom guilt had her lifting all eighty-plus pounds of him, front legs first, then followed by back legs. Not the easiest thing, especially when Fred was slippery from dancing in the waves.

The belt *clicked.* The door closed.

Ben turned to face her.

She'd expected questions about why she'd gone quiet. Instead, he'd just sat next to her, no pressure, no stress, and watched the sunset with her and Fred.

God, she liked him too freaking much.

She was firmly in cling mode—as in, wanting to cling to him forever.

His fingers brushed her cheek, and she realized she'd been staring. "Did you want me to drive?" he asked.

"No," she said. "I'm fine. I've got it."

Deep brown eyes on hers. "That's not what I asked."

She replayed her answer, his question, then bit back a smile. "You remember."

She'd complained about hating to drive on the way to the beach, lamenting the traffic on her circuit of doggy day care, lab, back to doggy day care, and finally back home, and how with Bay Area traffic, it took longer than a reasonable human being should have to deal with.

His eyes flared, but he didn't say anything other than, "I remember."

"Do you mind?"

Another flash. "I wouldn't have offered if I did."

This man . . . was confusing and wonderful and . . . confusing. "Do you really mean it?"

"Stef." His hands cupped her cheeks. *"I wouldn't have offered if I minded."*

Thud.

Thud.

"Okay."

"That you understand I wouldn't have offered if I minded, or that you want me to drive?"

After considering that for a moment, she said, "Both."

A flash of bright white teeth. He plucked the keys from her fingers, threaded his arm through hers, and led her around the hood of the car, opening the passenger's side door, then waiting for her to sit before buckling her in.

"Thank you," she whispered.

He cupped her cheek, held her gaze. "You're welcome."

Then he got into the driver's seat, having to wrestle with the controls for a few minutes to try and fit his long legs in her tiny Prius. But then he was in, and the car was on, and he drove her home.

———

"THIS ISN'T what I had in mind when I told you I'd buy you dinner," she said, setting the paper plates and napkins on the coffee table alongside the pizza that had just been delivered.

She'd been thinking fancy restaurant, candles and table-cloths, and soft music in the background.

Not necessarily because she liked those things.

But because he lived in a penthouse and owned a building in SF. He was probably used to fancy shit. Hell, he had that white rug where anyone might just stain it.

Then again, he'd gone to the small theater, walked on that sticky floor, and shared popcorn and a KitKat.

That wasn't exactly fancy.

Neither was eating pizza and drinking beers.

But that's what he'd suggested when his stomach had rumbled on the drive home, and she'd ordered the food on the app, so it had arrived almost when they did.

Ben opened the lid, inhaled deeply. "Fuck, that smells good."

Her pussy clenched.

As though he felt it, Ben glanced over at her, and she got lost in the heat in his eyes. He closed the pizza box, prowling over to her. Her nostrils flared, and she didn't back up when he stepped right into her space, sharing her air. "You have condoms?" he asked.

So not the most romantic of statements.

But also the same question she'd been asking herself.

The answer to which had her cursing internally.

"No," she breathed.

His eyes slid to half-mast, and though she detected the

disappointment there, the same that she was feeling (why, seriously, didn't she have an emergency condom? Also, why didn't *he* have one?) He didn't say anything, just trailed his knuckles down her throat, halting at the neckline of the sweatshirt.

Then he took her hand and tugged her over to the couch, a plate laden with pizza plunked into her lap a moment later.

He was beside her in the next, pizza on his plate.

But neither of them ate.

Fingers on her throat again, another shiver wracking her frame. "Stop looking at me like that," he rasped.

Her lips parted, a shuddering breath escaping. "I can't help it."

His plate hit the table.

His hands slid into her hair. His lips came down—

Fred launched himself onto the couch . . . and snatched a slice of pizza off her plate.

She was so in Ben's thrall that it took her a moment to realize what Fred had done. Gasping, she jumped to her feet, Ben somehow managing to snag her plate before she dumped it on the ground.

"Fred!" she snapped, taking a step after her pooch, but the little asshole had already eaten the slice.

Stef couldn't believe he'd done that.

She'd already fed him, and she'd broken him of the counter-surfing for food habit when he was a puppy, and he'd never been much of a food-snatcher, least of all right off her lap.

And the turd didn't even have the common courtesy to look guilty.

He just licked his lips.

"I—I—"

Ben started laughing, setting her plate on the table, before crossing the room to crouch in front of Fred.

Everything inside her went tense for one moment.

She didn't know this man, and if he did something to Fred . .

.

He reached a hand out to her dog, stroked his fingers over fluffy, golden ears. "That was naughty," Ben murmured in a voice that made her want to be naughty herself. "Pizza will make you sick."

Fred had stilled, staring up at him.

"You can't do that again, got it?" Ben ordered, firmer now. "No stealing food. No pizza."

Fred whined and sank down onto his belly.

Apparently satisfied, Ben stood up, crossed back to the table, put another slice onto her plate, then came to her and tugged her down next to him on the couch. "Now then," he said. "No more looking at me. Just eat."

She opened her mouth.

"*Eat*," he ordered.

She took the plate he shoved at her but didn't pick up her pizza. Instead, she grabbed the remote, shoved it at *him*, then snagged her cell.

"Stef." Another order.

Well, good thing she knew how to give orders herself . . . or at least with Ben she found that she could.

"You find something to watch," she told him. "And I'm using Instacart to *order*"—heh—"us some condoms."

His gaze shot to hers.

A grin, wicked and so different from what he'd given to her before. Different in a good way, in the *best* way.

She folded his fingers over the remote. "Put something on."

Another hot look, but then he turned on the TV, she got busy on the app, and by the time their delivery showed up, the pizza was gone, a nerdy Sci-Fi horror flick was watched, and . . . then Ben put something *else* on.

And it was glorious.

CHAPTER TWENTY

Ben

SHE WAS asleep next to him, her breathing slow and steady.

Lips reddened from his kisses, her lipstick long since rubbed off. Beautiful and cute and sweet and . . . funny.

That had surprised him as she'd watched the movie, droll commentary interjecting their viewing. She'd been quiet in the theater, and when he'd asked her why, she'd only said that she could talk over previews but never over the sacredness of a movie in a theater.

Either way—*both* ways—he liked her.

A lot.

He liked her body just as much, her personality to equal measure. Hell, he'd burst out laughing when she'd looked up from her phone as he'd paused his scrolling through the selections on the streaming platform, bent to look over her shoulder, and pointed to the screen, lips curving in a self-deprecating smile, joking, "Magnum. Definitely get magnum."

"Boys and their penises," she'd teased, rolling her eyes, and running with the joke.

Because he wasn't magnum, not that he gave a shit, and

when the condoms had arrived, they weren't either. But he just liked making her smile, even if the joke was at his expense.

Plus, he'd still made good use of the condoms, no matter the size.

After chuckling his ass off when she'd smirked and said, "Big hands. Big . . . Sci-Fi nerd."

Laughter, so much of it over the last two days, and he knew that his decision to pursue this was the right one.

She was the right one.

He smoothed her hair off her face, smiling as she nuzzled closer, her arms tightening around him. Even sweet in her sleep.

Ben let his eyes slide close, pondered his next move, determined to negotiate the weeks and months and hopefully *years* ahead with Stef like a business deal and not like he'd normally handle a relationship with a woman.

He wasn't going to be tentative.

He was playing to win.

━━━━━

HE'D JUST DRIFTED off to sleep when Stef jerked up in his arms.

"Sweetheart!"

"What?" he asked, sitting up next to her. "What's the matter?"

"Sweetheart," she said again, spinning in his arms to stare up at him. "We forgot about Sweetheart, and she's probably hungry and has to go to the bathroom." Guilt slid across her face. "She's probably terrified and—"

"Baby," he said, cupping her jaw, feeling a piece of his heart break off, drift through the air, and float to her. It was hers. And probably not just that one part of it. "She's fine."

Stef's hand clamped over his. "You haven't been back—"

"My assistant came and picked her up this morning." He smiled gently. "She's fine. I need to get her tomorrow"—his eyes flicked to the clock on the nightstand—"or later today, actually. But they're getting along fine. Claire even said that she hasn't tried to bite anyone."

Stef relaxed. "Your assistant is watching your dog?"

A nod as he coaxed her down to the mattress. "Well, technically, she'll be my newest VP on Monday—tomorrow, that is. The important thing is that she's fine, Sweetheart is fine, and you can go back to sleep."

A few blinks, her sleep-hazed and half-panicked mind processing his words.

"Your VP has your dog?"

He nodded, biting back a grin as he smoothed back her hair again.

"Okay," she murmured, nuzzling close, and it wasn't three more heartbeats before she was out again.

So fucking cute.

———

SHE WAS LESS cute in the morning.

Mostly because they were in an argument.

Okay, who was he kidding? She was fucking adorable, dwarfed in his shirt, her arms crossed over her breasts, as one bare foot stomped on the floor.

Fred whined, his food in his dish.

"I'm not bringing Sweetheart here," he said, for what must have been the fifth time since he'd told Stef he needed to retrieve Sweetheart soon.

"You are." There that foot went again.

"Sweetheart isn't good with other dogs."

"You said she wasn't good with people," she pointed out. "But she was good with me, and Fred is the therapy dog at doggy day care. If a pup is having a bad day, they put it with Fred, and he gets them through the nerves."

"Sweetheart doesn't have nerves."

Her nostrils flared. Her lips pressed flat. "Ben," she said. "I'd like to spend more time with you. That would be easier if our dogs got along. It's not like you can ask . . ." Her eyes slid to the side then back to his as she remembered Claire's name. "*Claire* to dog sit all the time."

"It's not—" He broke off when a flash of pain slid through her eyes, and he was struggling to process it when she spoke again.

"I'll go change." A smile that was *not* normal, even based on the limited time he'd known her. "Let you get your shirt, so you can get out of here."

If the smile wasn't normal, then her tone was . . . peculiar.

Off.

Shut down.

And then she was gone, spinning and striding down the hall. The door to the bedroom *clicked* closed.

He looked at Fred. "What was that?"

The pooch just lay down by his food dish, head resting on his paws.

Ben didn't have time to process the tone and smile any further because the bedroom door opened, and Stef came out in a pair of black leggings and a loose sweatshirt. Her eyes met his, and that smile made another appearance.

Silently, she handed him his shirt.

But she was obvious about not letting her fingers brush his, and as soon as she passed it to him, she turned away and went to the sink, starting to wash the dishes from the simple breakfast she'd made them.

A bagel.

Enough cream cheese to clog his arteries.

Delicious with a bit of spice, and he'd eaten the entire thing, along with two cups of coffee.

None of that, however, explained the change in Stef.

Still, he knew there weren't that many dishes, so instead of storming over and demanding that she talk to him, he did what he might do if someone was trying to negotiate him out of a deal.

He waited.

Silently.

And eventually, she ran out of things to clean. Though, he had to give her credit; once the dishes ran out, she moved to wiping down the counter, the table, the sink, even the fridge, and inside its glass shelves.

She closed the fridge, turned around, and froze.

As though having expected him to be out the door.

"What's going on?" he asked.

Another flash in her eyes before they flicked over his shoulder. "I'll help you get your stuff together so you can go. Do you need a ride?"

"My car's here," he said, taking a step to the right to block her path when she would have slid by him.

"Okay, good. I'll just get your keys."

Wrong. *Wrong.*

This was so wrong.

He snagged her arm before she could disappear down that hall. "What is it?"

She tugged her arm free.

Fuck that. He scooped her up in his arms, carried her to the couch, and sat down with her in his lap.

"What are you doing?" she asked, squirming in his hold.

"What are *you* doing?" he retorted, tightening it. "Why are you freezing me out? Are you that mad about the dogs?"

"No, of course not," she said, and her tone told him that was the truth.

But there was something else he'd missed, something he was going to get to the bottom of. So, while he wouldn't hold a business rival on his lap, he *would* hold them accountable, at least until he understood the motivations that went into the process.

And that was the part he was severely missing.

The motivation for Stef shutting down.

Not the dogs. Not the argument. She seemed to be having as much fun bickering as he had . . . until he'd said . . . *what?*

He couldn't pinpoint it.

She'd stopped squirming, going still on his lap, and Ben scrambled to tease out the answer to what he'd done.

He was no closer to the answer when she gave him a clue.

"Just go," she whispered.

And he remembered her talking about her friends, the light and happiness . . . and the way she'd said, *"How much I'm going to miss them when it's over."*

Over.

When it's over.

Not if it would end someday, but as though her friendships ending with them was a forgone conclusion.

And she'd come to the conclusion that he wanted things to be over.

Which couldn't be further from the truth.

But they'd known each other for no time at all. How could he possibly convince her that he wanted to see where this went?

That he wanted her, hopefully forever.

"Stef," he said. "I want to get to know you better, too."

"Right." A nod, her eyes meeting his just for a moment, but then they darted away again, drifted back down to her hands.

"You going anywhere today?"

Silence.

Then her lips pressed flat.

"Stef?"

"No," she whispered.

"I'll go take care of Sweetheart, drop her at my place, but I'm coming back."

"Right," she whispered again.

And he knew in that moment that words wouldn't mean much to her.

That was okay. He would just have to show it to her.

Carefully, he set her on the couch, patted Fred on his head, and gathered his things.

"I'll see you soon," he said, and kissed her forehead.

Another of those wrecked smiles, one that almost had him staying, but he knew that wouldn't show her anything, wouldn't prove anything. She needed to understand that he was going to come back. "Okay."

He'd show her that.

Because not once did he think she wouldn't be worth fighting for.

CHAPTER TWENTY-ONE

Stef

HE LEFT, the door clicking closed behind him.

Why had she ruined the loveliness, the good time they'd been having?

She'd pushed, and he'd left.

Oh, she knew that he'd promised to come back, but he wouldn't. She'd seen that look on his face, and it was familiar. It was something she'd seen over and over again. Plus, who would return to a woman who argued with him about something at hour . . . what? Thirty-six or so? Two dates in and already making demands. Waking him up in the middle of the night with her anxiety. Making him the only breakfast she could—both because she sucked at cooking and because all she'd had to offer were bagels and her cinnamon cream cheese and coffee. If she'd had time to shop, she could have made him muffins, but . . .

She sighed.

Add in a dog tagging along on dates, anxiety nightmares, picking a fight before nine in the morning.

The ideal woman she was.

"Okay, Yoda," she muttered, forcing herself to get up and lock the door, her heart squeezing when she saw that he'd turned the bolt on the knob, so it was already locked.

Dammit.

She should have hung on a little longer.

But all she could think was that it was better now than when she was even more involved.

When it would hurt more.

So maybe she *did* know why she'd taken the first opportunity to push him away, to pull back and protect herself. For all her talk of clinging to him, to absorbing as much of him as she possibly could, in the end, she'd chosen self-preservation.

Close down.

Protect whatever shred of herself that was left.

Probably the smartest thing she'd ever done, even if she hated the idea of never seeing Ben again.

Losing Chance had broken something in her. Her parents trying to cope with his suicide, his mental illness, and distancing themselves from her had broken something else. And then Jeremy. Who she'd thought was a fucking savior, that white knight on the horse sweeping in to save her.

She didn't have it in her.

She'd wanted to be brave and soak in every moment.

But when Ben had gotten that familiar look on his face, she'd known she couldn't.

Stef had snapped so quickly back into herself, a tape measure whirling back into its case, the metal ricocheting and biting at her fingers just before fully closing. It hurt, but it belonged there, just like her.

She'd had her fun, and it was done.

Fuck, that hurt.

But she only had herself to blame.

"Enough," she whispered, going to the fridge and getting on her meal prep for the week. She could slow cook chicken—

plunk some olive oil, salt, and pepper into the Crock-Pot, throw in the chicken, and forget about it for eight hours.

Then shred it, throw it into some bagged salad, and be done with it.

Not a gourmet cook, but she could make a few edible things, and luckily, she didn't mind eating the same thing day in and out.

She went through the motions of meal prepping for the week, of cleaning her house and giving Fred a bath—well, Fred got cleaned up first and was turned out into the back yard to run off his after-bath zoomies, and *then* she cleaned the house, including the trail of wet pawprints and hair that stretched from the bathroom to the slider.

What she didn't do was allow her mind to wander back to Ben.

Which meant she thought about him every minute.

And as the hours went by, the small tendril of hope she'd been holding on to, even knowing it was stupid as hell, faded.

"It's okay," she whispered.

She'd forget about Ben and move on, and all would be good.

"Right," she muttered, not believing herself, not even for a moment.

But she'd be okay, eventually.

Sighing, knowing it was the truth, she walked to the slider, intending to let Fred back in. It was getting late, and she needed to make dinner, get ready for work the next day, to figure out some way to not be sad.

Because she wasn't really ready for Heidi to see that she was pining for a man she couldn't have—

A knock at the front door pulled her from the slider.

She didn't even get halfway to it when she saw Ben's face appear in the sidelight, big brown eyes on hers.

Her feet slid to a stop, and she swallowed hard.

He held her gaze as he knocked again.

"Right," she whispered, moving to the door. Nothing had

changed, even if he'd come back this time. There would be a time when he wouldn't return or would tell her to go and . . .

She wasn't going to open that door.

She'd drawn her line in the sand.

He held up something in the window.

No, not *something*, but a fur baby. Sweetheart and her cute little black eyes peered through the glass, her white body looking so tiny in Ben's large hands.

And she knew she was fucked.

Her feet began moving, and she reached the door, hesitating again until there was another knock, Ben's voice saying, "It's cold out here."

"Right," she muttered, unlocking the door, knowing that she should just walk away and make him go back to his car.

But . . . Sweetheart.

But . . . Ben.

Her vulnerable, desperate heart wanted him for just a little longer.

She unlocked the door. Ben pushed it open.

Sweetheart wriggled her way out of his arms and into hers and began licking Stef's chin with enthusiasm. Not sleepy this time, not calmly cuddling after a burst of protectiveness. She was a writhing ball of fluff, and Stef found her heart squeezing, her lips turning up into a smile.

"Hi, baby," she murmured, stroking a hand down her back.

Her fur was so soft, and she couldn't help but cuddle her closer. Ben slipped by them when she was distracted, and it took her a moment to realize he'd made more than one trip.

A backpack. A crate. A tote bag printed with Sweetheart's face.

A paper bag with grease stains on the side.

The air filled with a delicious scent that went along with that paper bag, something fried, something that made her stomach, that had a week's worth of boring salads ahead of it, rumble.

She needed.

"Dinner," Ben said, unnecessarily.

"Right," she whispered.

He closed the door, locked it, and ran his knuckles down her throat. "How do we do this?"

For a moment, she thought he meant her and him.

Then she realized he meant how did they introduce the dogs to each other. "Let me grab Fred's leash." Just in case her boy got a little rambunctious. She shoved Sweetheart at Ben, reached into her wall organizer for Fred's leash, and then moved to the slider, opening it a fraction so that she could clip it to Fred's collar.

"Okay," she said. "You can let her down."

Ben's face was a study in concern, but he merely held her eyes for a second, as though reading her resolve, and then he nodded and put Sweetheart on the floor.

Please, let this go okay.

Sweetheart glanced around then her gaze came to her, to Fred.

And . . . it went horribly.

She sprinted over toward Fred, barking and snarling and becoming the beast Ben had accused her of being. But this wasn't Stef's first rodeo. She held tight to Fred's leash, positioned herself between them, and waited for Sweetheart to reach them.

She'd already slowed by the time she came within five feet.

Then stopped at three feet away, her body quivering in fear this time.

Fred didn't pull at the leash, just slumped to the floor in a movement that made Sweetheart jump and growl.

Silence filled the room, Sweetheart eyeing Fred like he was evil incarnate.

Then she tentatively took a step forward.

Fred didn't move, merely opened one eye as she took another, and then another until they were nose-to-nose and Sweetheart was sniffing delicately. Fred huffed out a breath, flopping to the side and making her jump again, minus the growl this time. He held perfectly still as Sweetheart made her way around him, sniffing every blade of hair, it seemed.

Her eyes came to Stef's, and Stef slowly reached a hand down to scratch Fred then her little head.

Sweetheart rumbled in contentment this time.

For just a moment before she surprised everyone but seemingly herself, and curled up between Fred's outstretched legs, a tiny white ball amongst golden fur. Another contented hum, her eyes closing. Fred glanced at Stef, who gave him and Sweetheart another scratch. Then, he too, shut his lids.

"I'll be damned," Ben murmured.

Stef set down his leash, making sure to stay within reach, just in case there was an issue, but her gut told her there wouldn't be.

Not with how relaxed Fred was.

"He shares your superpower?"

A little smug crept into her expression, and she didn't bother to stifle it, "Told you."

He smiled. "And rightly so, apparently." A beat. "Remind me to never doubt you again." He held up the bag of food. "Can I make it up to you with dinner?"

She stared at the bag, at the items in the hall.

Ben shifted a little closer. "I told you I was going to come back."

"But for how long?"

He went so still that it only took her a second to realize that she hadn't said that in her head as she'd intended. Oh no, she'd said it out loud. God, she'd said it *out loud,* revealing too much.

Ben set the bag on the table.

Her heart thudded, and she took a step backward, but he was already there, snagging her hand, drawing her over to the couch, turning her so that the backs of her legs hit the couch, pressing down on her shoulder until she sat.

"I'm going to tell you a story," he said.

She inhaled.

"It's not a happy story, and it's not the kind of thing I share with anyone." Her fingertips tingled, pulse pounding in her veins. "And I want you to know that I've never told anyone all of it."

Trust.

He was trusting her with something that made him vulnerable.

The magnitude of that sat heavy on her chest, her tongue, her throat.

"Okay?"

She nodded, managed to force out "Okay" back.

"In all my enjoyment of hearing you talk yesterday, I didn't get around to telling you what I do," he said. "I'm the CEO of Hunt Inc. I started the business, grew it, still chair the board, and am now the majority shareholder."

Her eyes went wide.

Hunt was . . . big.

Like owning the most popular social media apps and search engines and delving into video and TV and movies big. They'd been fairly small until the previous year, and now they were on the stock exchange and had gone global.

Last she'd heard, Hunt owned the most downloaded app in the U.S., U.K., India, and was expanding to Europe and China.

From blowing up the stock market to dominating world-wide in just three months.

Their independent movies had been popular for years, had won all those fancy awards, but the movie he'd taken her to see in the theater on Friday, *that* was their first big blockbuster, a film that was threatening to break opening weekend records—at least for a film that wasn't a superhero flick.

"Most of Hunt's success has come from the people below me who are smart and talented and have built it with me brick by brick," he said, his hands resting on his thighs. "But the rest has come from me both being open to new ventures and also from me being a stubborn ass by refusing to jump into some when I didn't feel like they were worth the risk."

Her lips opened, closed, not sure what to say.

"I love the company," he went on. "I've literally bled for it, but in the eight years I've been building it, I have always followed my instincts—even when people said I was a dumbass to do so."

"Ben," she began, still not sure what to say.

"And then three months ago, I got to where I wanted, and I felt . . . empty. My parents are gone, and I'd built Hunt for them, to show them I could be something, could make them proud." He laughed humorlessly. "But I didn't have anyone to share it with. Then Claire downloaded Tinder." His lips twitched. "Maybe I need to get Hunt into singles apps?"

She found herself chuckling. "Maybe."

"So, she downloaded it onto my phone without me knowing, set up a profile, and . . . then you swiped."

Her throat went tight. "I told you that I thought you were the most beautiful man I'd ever seen," she whispered. "But I had to get good and drunk to get up the courage to swipe."

"Well," he said. "I'm glad you were drinking that night."

Stef nibbled on her bottom lip. "What did you think when you saw the notification?"

"That I wanted to kiss that sexy mouth of yours."

"Oh."

He lightly bopped her nose. "Yeah. *Oh.*" A grin. "Then I was furious with Claire for doing it. She was the only one at the time with access to my phone," he added. "That has now changed— my password and passcode, that is—so there won't be any more downloads. Speaking of which, you need to set one up on your phone."

Her nose wrinkled under his finger. "Not you, too. I hate having to type in my code every time I want to use my phone."

"We'll talk about that later," he said with just enough pushiness that she frowned. But then he began talking again, distracting her. "My instincts said you were different, that there was something special about you."

Special?

Um . . .

"I—"

"But I'm not great with women. I'm a geek who loves fantasy and Sci-Fi. I was a skinny geek until a few years ago when I started working out because I . . ." His lips pressed flat. "I didn't have anything better to do. I spent my life being gangly and thin and not fitting my body. I'm not used to women giving me a second glance—or at least one that was due to the way I looked and not because they want a slice of Hunt."

She reached for him, covered his hand, realized the callouses on them were from the hard work he put into the gym. "I'm not . . . I'm not like that—" Not special. Not after his money.

"I know." A beat. "Why do you think I didn't delete the app?"

"I . . ." She shook her head. "I don't know. It just seems like we don't fit. You're gorgeous and successful, and . . . I'm me. I work at a lab. I live in a condo, not a penthouse. We don't make sense." Another shake. "Hell, my longest relationship with a male is with Fred."

His eyes flicked over to Fred and Sweetheart, now both soundly sleeping, and his mouth curved up.

"I don't care about your past relationships or where you work or that you don't think you're absolutely the sexiest woman I've ever had the privilege of touching." His hand found hers. "I don't care that you live in a condo or that you like a God-awful amount of cream cheese on your bagels." A squeeze. "I care that you love Fred and have weekly beach days with him. I care that you liked the movie on Friday and were fine just staying in, cuddling on the couch, and watching a show last night. I care that you kiss me like you mean it and that you worried about Sweetheart."

He came a little closer, and her heart thumped at the intensity in his gaze. "I like you, Stef. For real. More than I should, considering the amount of time we've spent together, but I'm not backing off. I thought I'd messed up my chance with you three months ago, so to have this with you, now . . . I'm not just going to walk away."

God, how she'd dreamed of such words.

God, how she wished she could believe them now.

Ben, apparently, could see that.

He touched her cheek. "I know that words are hard to trust," he said. "Trust me, I've been around enough people to understand that. So"—his lips brushed hers—"I'm just going to show you that I'm not going anywhere." Another brush. "Unless you want me to go."

She'd spent the day building up armor around her heart, trying to ignore the pain of Ben leaving, of not being able to explore this thing between them, attempting to pretend it was for the best.

And after all that angst, one thing was critically clear.

She didn't want him to go.

The part of her that still had hope, held tight to his words, his promise of showing her he'd stick around.

Maybe it was stupid.

But he was here and so earnest and . . . she wanted him, wanted this man.

"So, can you do something for me?"

Her stomach clenched, waiting for the other shoe to drop.

"Can you just give me a chance to prove I'm going to stick around?"

God, she liked this man *so* much.

So much that she felt her heart grow lighter, felt as though she could actually do this, and . . . she found herself teasing.

"That depends."

His eyes warmed. "On what?"

"On two things, actually."

He just lifted his brows and waited for her to speak.

"First, on what's in the bag?"

Wordlessly, he snagged it, opened it to show her two delicious-smelling cheeseburgers and an obscene amount of French fries.

Okay, that passed.

The cocky grin Ben shot her confirmed that he knew she was thinking that.

"What's the second?" he asked.

"You let me pick what we watch."

His smile now was soft, his fingers on her cheek gentle. "Done," he murmured.

And Stef had the feeling that she was *done,* too.

Done for *him.*

CHAPTER TWENTY-TWO

Ben

THE DOGS SLEPT CURLED TOGETHER on the bed in the front room.

Stef had dozed off a couple of minutes ago in his arms.

The show blared on TV.

Stargate.

He nearly laughed at remembering her quoting all those lines, her sighing obsession with the colonel who'd eventually become a general obvious.

But Ben hadn't minded, not in the least, not when she was cuddled up next to him, her steady breath on his neck, her arms wrapped tightly around him. She stirred, and he knew he should tuck her into bed, take himself and Sweetheart home, but he'd brought all the gear hoping to get the invite to stay the night.

The thought of going back to his place, to his empty bed and that cold, large space wasn't appealing.

"Ben?" she murmured, running her nose across his throat.

"Hmm?" he murmured back, sliding his hand gently up and down her back. She shivered, and fuck, he loved when she did that.

"Will you stay?"

He felt like fist-pumping, had to physically lock down the *whoop* inside him. "Of course," he said once he could manage not sounding too much like an idiot.

"Mmm," was her only response.

Smiling, he kept his hand moving, settling her further, waiting until her breathing had gone deep and slow again before carefully sitting up and carrying her into the bedroom.

The pups got up and followed him, Sweetheart trailing Fred, and he half-expected Fred to jump into bed ahead of him. Stef had teased him earlier about him having spent the previous evening sleeping in Fred's spot, and that Fred wouldn't stand for it. But the pooch barely even glanced at him as he went to the corner of the room and lay down on the cushy bed in the corner, Sweetheart right behind him.

After tucking Stef into bed, he moved to his bag in the front room, retrieving his phone and charger, finding a spare plug back in the bedroom to set it charging.

She was out, burrowed into the blankets, and he crawled into bed behind her, feeling another piece of his heart flow to her when she immediately rolled and burrowed into his embrace.

He wasn't a man who liked cuddling.

But he didn't think he'd be able to sleep without Stef in his arms.

———

COFFEE ROUSED HIM.

Along with Stef crawling back into bed on top of him.

Her hands slid along his bare skin, pulling him out of the fog of sleep, doing the remainder of the job that the coffee hadn't. He was hard already, not an uncommon morning occurrence, except *this* morning Stef's hands were on his body, and he was granite, a throbbing pulse of need.

"Morning," she whispered, her mouth pressing to his jaw, drifting down his throat, along his abdomen, tiny torturing presses of her mouth slowly moving down toward the waistband of his boxer briefs.

She tugged the material out of the way, and without warning, sucked his cock into her mouth.

Deeply.

His curse was garbled, his voice barely recognizable to his own ears, and then he cursed again when her hand joined the party, stroking as she sucked, and fuck . . . just that quickly he was seconds away from exploding.

Reaching under her armpits, he yanked her up his body, stealing her mouth in a scorching kiss as he wrestled the blankets to the side and flipped them so she was beneath him. Her eyes blazed and she'd changed, was wearing just a soft, fuzzy robe that had parted from his movements, revealing so much pale skin that his mouth watered with the need to taste.

"Are you wearing anything underneath this?" he asked roughly, trailing a hand up her side.

Her teeth nibbled at her bottom lip, a wicked gleam in her eyes. "Why don't you find out?"

That was a request he wouldn't deny.

His fingers shook as he undid the robe.

Spoiler alert: she wasn't wearing anything.

"Fuck," he groaned, his gaze tracing over her body, cock twitching when her stare drifted down, too, and he wondered if the sight had her on the razor's edge of control, like it had his—catching on the tips of her breasts, hardened and desperate for his mouth, then lower over the curve of her stomach he wanted to kiss his way across, then down to the flare of her hips. He wondered if the sight of his hand as it slipped between her thighs fractured her control to wisps like his.

"Fuck," she echoed, legs spreading wider.

She was wet. He'd known that even before he touched her, could see it gathering on her skin, coating the insides of her thighs, allowing his fingers to slide through the hot, silken folds of her labia easily.

Her face was stark with desire, jaw clenching, eyes flared bright.

He slipped one thick finger inside her.

Gasping, Stef threw her head back on the pillows, her hips bucked against his hand, bucking again when he dragged his thumb over her clit.

"That's it," he murmured, bending and sucking her nipple.

Deeply and without warning.

Partly because he couldn't stop himself. Partly because she liked it a little rough.

Drawing deeply, he let her cries wash over him, didn't gentle, didn't yield, not even when her back arched up off the mattress, legs going even wider. He needed more. He needed her—to be in her and on top of her, pressed to her soft body, her curves soft to his hard. He needed to be fucking her fast and furious and—

Her hips arched up, and he felt all that silken heat against the tip of his cock.

His control withered away.

Her hips tilted a second time, brushing against him, calling for him to thrust, to plant himself deep.

He pulled away.

Stef cursed, reached for him.

But he was already stretching for the nightstand, for the box of condoms, grabbing one and tearing it open with his teeth, rolling it down his cock. Then he was stroking deep.

This wasn't slow or controlled.

It was fast and frenzied, a frantic race to the end, a baton pass, him trying to get her there before he exploded. Stef doing the same for him. Her hands didn't stop moving on him, gripping tight to his shoulders, his ass, gripping him tight inside, too. Over and over he plunged into the tight, wet heat of her pussy, riding that razor's edge, so damned close to exploding—

And then her breathing hitched.

Her neck arched.

She clenched around him as she came.

One more thrust and Ben was done, his orgasm barreling up and down his spine, sending heat and pleasure to his fingers, down to his toes.

He collapsed, barely able to prop himself on his elbows, chest heaving, sweat dripping down his spine. "Fuck, you're beautiful," he murmured, summoning enough energy to roll to the side, to keep her close as he stroked a hand up and down her side.

Her lips curved, but thankfully, she didn't argue with him over the compliment, just kept her eyes closed and snuggled into him.

Fuck, he loved when she did that.

He held her closer, enjoyed the feel of her slowing breathing on his throat before he managed to roll away from her, to pull up his boxer briefs, to move to the bathroom and take care of the condom then make his way to the kitchen.

To the coffee pot.

He filled two mugs, added cream and sugar to Stef's—his, he took black—and then made his way to the bedroom.

But not before he saw Fred and Sweetheart standing outside in the back yard, staring at him through the glass, sad puppy eyes on full display. "I'll be right there," he said before walking down the hall, knowing that Stef must have let them out before she'd come and attacked him.

In the best way possible.

He handed Stef the mug, turned back for the kitchen, and started taking care of the dogs' food. He'd seen Fred's intricate food prep the day before and had done his best to replicate it when Stef came out of the bedroom, her sexy robe pulled around her again, though now that he knew she didn't wear anything beneath it, she was even more of a temptation.

Ben wanted her.

He'd just had her.

But he wanted to be buried balls deep in her again.

"You're making Fred's breakfast?" she murmured, coming close and glancing over his shoulder, her breasts pressing into his arm.

"Trying to," he said. "Did I do it right?"

Her gaze flicked over the bowl and then she smiled. "Yup," she said, breaking up a piece of chicken he hadn't apparently shredded small enough, sprinkling it over the kibble. "Thank you." She rose on tiptoe, pressed a kiss to his cheek. "You didn't have to do that, or bring me the coffee."

God, had that asshole who she'd dated not taken care of her at all?

But all he said was, "I wanted to."

Her mouth curved, and she squeezed his arm before going to the slider and letting in Fred, bending as though to scoop up Sweetheart.

But Sweetheart dodged away.

"Hang on," Stef said. "We should be careful with—"

He'd already set the food dish down and didn't process what she'd said until her voice went a little panicked. Then he realized there were two dogs heading for Fred's bowl, and Sweetheart wasn't good at sharing.

Shit.

He tried to scoop the bowl up, but he didn't beat the dogs to it, and then there were two heads in the stainless-steel container.

Gut clenching, he turned to snatch up Sweetheart—

"Wait," Stef said, coming over.

Ben froze, blinking at the sight. Sweetheart took a handful of bites and then laid down next to the bowl, letting Fred finish the rest.

Letting Fred.

What the hell had the witch done to his dog?

Sweetheart was practically civilized now.

Stef put a few more kibbles in, since Sweetheart had apparently found her breakfast in Fred's, and then Fred ate until the bowl was empty before flopping down next to Sweetheart, alternating between licking the container and his pup-friend's ear.

"You're amazing," Ben told her as she came to his side.

"No," she whispered. "That's Fred. All Fred."

He thought she was wrong. That it was her—all her.

And he looked forward to proving it.

CHAPTER TWENTY-THREE

Stef

"OH. MY. GOD." A beat. "You got laid."

Despite herself, she felt her cheeks heat, knowing that Heidi was clearly able to see that Stef had, in fact, gotten laid.

Multiple times.

With multiple glorious orgasms.

So glorious that she was a little sore as she meandered her way into the lab. Meandered because Heidi was there, and Stef knew her friend would notice the difference. Hell, when she'd looked in the mirror that morning, she'd hardly recognized her own face.

Happy.

She'd looked utterly happy.

And had decided it was a good look on her.

That had been after her momentary panic with the food dish and the two pups, of course. She hadn't thought Fred would get possessive, but he was so much bigger than Sweetheart, could easily hurt her, so she'd worried.

But then, like two peas in a pod, it hadn't been an issue in the least.

Then Ben had made her a bagel, with loads of cream cheese, had downed a second cup of coffee, and disappeared into the bathroom to shower and change, coming out in a suit that had taken her breath away.

"I thought you tech guys didn't wear suits."

He'd merely grinned, kissed the top of her head. "I'm glad you like it." Then he'd told her he had a meeting with the board that day, so he had dressed up for the occasion. Though from the glimpse she'd gotten of his closet Friday night, she knew that he was no stranger to a suit.

The entire back wall of his wardrobe had been filled with suits.

Now, Heidi squealed and clapped her hands together. "Yes! You got the best kind of laid."

Stef bit her lip. She had.

"Who is he? What does he look like? Where did you meet him? What did you do? How many times did you—"

Stef held up her hand. Not only to thwart the pure onslaught of questions but also in order to cut off Heidi. They were at work, for God's sake, and she wasn't going to spill her guts when an intern could come in at any point. "We're not talking about this right now."

Heidi started to protest.

The lab door opened.

Stef lifted her brows, silently telling her friend, "See?"

Heidi just lifted her hands in surrender as their newest intern walked in then issued some instructions to Stef and Aarav, before strolling over to her computer.

Aarav, quiet, shy—and did she mention quiet?—merely said, "Good morning."

Then they all got to work.

Stef on going over some data from the weekend, mostly seeing if their equipment was functioning properly, but also prepping some things for an experiment that Heidi wanted to conduct later in the week.

Her job probably wasn't exciting from the outside—spending her time going over spreadsheets and spectrometer readings—but she enjoyed the challenge of working with atoms, with trying to discover their secrets, trying to study something that couldn't be seen with the naked eye, with a normal microscope . . . hell, with *any* microscope.

It was all theory and testing and studying the blank spaces left behind. Atoms were too small to be able to see, so they studied the reactions between molecules more than the small, basic units of life themselves.

The ultimate puzzle.

And she was thrilled that she got to work on it, even her small part of it.

Her cell buzzed, and she glanced down at the screen quickly, knowing that she needed to turn it off and unable to believe she'd left it on. It could mess with the equipment, for one, and was a general distraction, for another.

But it wasn't Ben texting, as she'd hoped.

It was from . . . Heidi.

On a scale of one to a million, how good was it?

Stef glared.

Deliberately held up her cell, the screen facing her boss as she turned it off. But then because she was so fucking happy, she found herself mouthing, "A million and one."

Heidi grinned.

Stef slid her cell back into her pocket.

Then she let her life happy bleed into her work happy . . . and found herself *happy* happy for the first time in a long time.

———

SHE WAS DRIVING to doggy day care when Ben called her.

"Hello?" she answered via her car's Bluetooth.

"You done with work?"

"Just finished." She glanced over her shoulder, checked for traffic as she changed lanes.

"Come to my place."

Four husky words and her legs pressed together, her brain struggled to focus on the traffic clogging the freeway. "I have to go get Fred."

"Get Fred. Then come to my place."

Signaling again, she forced her way into the next lane, one step closer to the exit. "You have a white rug."

Silence.

Then, "Yes, I do."

"Right," she said, half-distracted as she crammed her car into a tiny opening and managed to navigate onto the off-ramp. Fucking California traffic was the worst.

"I'm not understanding your obsession with my white rug."

She thought it was rather obvious. "It can get dirty."

Another pause, shorter this time. "Isn't that what rugs do?"

Okay, he had her there. But still, it was a white rug and Fred was Fred. He'd get into something, and the white rug wouldn't be white and—

"Stef?"

She turned right at the signal. "Yeah?"

"It's just a rug."

He also had her there. Except, "It's probably an expensive rug, and you haven't seen what kind of damage a golden retriever can do to expensive *and* white household objects. He'll ruin it, and it's probably not washable, and I certainly can't afford to buy you a new one and—"

"Baby?"

The endearment had her heart fluttering up into her throat. "Yeah?" she managed to push out for a second time.

"Come to my place. Bring Fred."

Her protests welled again, but he just hung up.

Well, that was one way to end a conversation, and she found

that she wasn't even mad that he'd just disconnected. It was bossy and a little annoying but also a whole lot sexy, and . . . he wanted her to bring Fred.

That had her smiling and staring out the windshield.

A knock on the window had her jumping, clamping her hand to her chest. She hadn't realized that she'd made it into the drive-through pickup for day care, and Fred was there, a handler holding his leash.

She scrambled to unlock the doors, made small talk as Fred was buckled into his seat belt.

Just before she was going to pull away from the curb, her phone buzzed.

With a text from Ben.

Then again with another.

The first was a pin for her to navigate to the proper entrance of the parking garage. The second was a QR code for her to show the security office.

A final buzz told her to park in spot PH-3.

Stef stared blankly at her screen for a few minutes before Fred whined. That snapped her out of it, and she drove forward, pulling out of the lot and heading back for the freeway. She'd still need to stop at her place to feed Fred. He might be happy to see Sweetheart, but he wouldn't be thrilled for his dinner to be late—meaning arriving later than five minutes after she walked through the door at home.

Her phone rang again.

"Yes?" she said, seeing that it was Ben.

"I have food for Fred."

The signal turned red, and she slid to a stop, struggling to find the words. The directions. The gate pass. The parking spot. Food for Fred. It was too much. She didn't know what to say.

And Ben seemed to understand that.

"Hope you had a good day, baby," he said, right as the light turned green.

She waited as the cars in front of her moved then slowly

accelerated, heading north on 101 to make her way into the city. But even though she drove carefully, checked traffic, and made her way through the on-ramp and merging, her heart was pounding. Why was he doing all of this?

I'm just going to show you that I'm not going anywhere.

Remembering his words didn't slow her pulse. They only made her grip the steering wheel a little tighter.

"Stef?"

She swallowed hard, cleared her throat. "Yeah?"

"Did you have a good day?"

She was a smart woman. Some might even say smarter than average, but it took her much longer than average to process those words. But as though he'd sensed that, Ben waited patiently for her to answer. "I did." She cleared her throat again when it came out raspy. "Did you?"

"I did, baby. Thanks for asking."

"I—"

He waited.

She had too many thoughts and emotions roiling within her to give voice to them all, to give voice to even one of them. Her mind was a whirling dervish—Fred, directions, pass, dinner last night, Sweetheart, coffee, kisses, and—

"I'll see you soon," she eventually murmured.

"Okay, Stef. Drive safe."

They hung up, and she crawled her way through the traffic. Toward Ben.

And for the first time in her life, she had to wonder if she'd finally found herself moving in the right direction.

CHAPTER TWENTY-FOUR

Ben

THE SECURITY OFFICE had called up the moment Stef drove through the gate, giving him time to take the elevator down to the garage.

She parked next to his SUV and his sedan, her tiny little hybrid's back seat full to the brim of Fred's fuzzy, golden body.

He waited until she opened the driver's side door then stepped close.

"Ben," she whispered.

"Hi," he said, brushing back her hair. "Want me to get Fred?"

A nod. "O-okay."

He wrangled the pooch while she reached in for her purse, and by the time both doors were shut, Stef seemed a little more relaxed. Enough, at least, to lean close and kiss him on the cheek. "Hi."

"You good?"

Her eyes were soft. "Yeah."

"Good," he said, slipping his arm around her and leading her toward the elevators.

"How did your meeting go?"

His heart squeezed that she'd remembered, that she'd asked. "Typical bullshit. No big problems, but endless droning on."

"Meetings," she said on a sigh.

"You have your fair share?"

"Unfortunately." A smile. "Though, Heidi has more of them than me, much to her chagrin."

Heidi her boss. Heidi her friend.

"When am I going to meet your friends?"

Her steps hitched, and she glanced up at him. "You want to meet my friends?"

Again. He wanted to murder that fucker, Jeremy. To have deposited the insecurity so deeply into her, who'd had her doubting that he wanted to do something as simple as meeting her friends, who'd had her shocked that Ben remembered how she took her coffee or would make breakfast for her and her dog.

At first, he'd looked at Stef and had seen red lips and curves.

Then he chatted online with her and thought she was funny and smart, someone he wanted to know better.

So getting to meet her in person, seeing how sweet and lovely she was, then knowing that someone had dimmed that, made her doubt herself, absolutely killed him. Especially when he got those glimpses of her humor, of the fire that was often banked inside her, and he knew that if she hadn't been smothered, they would be there all the time.

That she wouldn't still be carrying all those shadows in her eyes.

The elevator doors opened, and he ushered her onto the cart, punching in the code that would take the car up to his floor, asking, "Are they important to you?"

"My friends?"

He nodded.

Her teeth pressed into her bottom lip, a flash of white digging into red. "Yes, of course they are."

"Then I want to meet them."

Her throat worked, and she released her bottom lip. "I . . ."

He shifted Fred's leash to the other hand so he could cup her cheek. "I want to meet them, but only if you're okay with it."

A pause, her eyes searching his until the elevator opened up into his entryway. He held the door as they stepped off, and then her gaze came back to his, studying until Sweetheart heard them and came running.

Fred wiggled like he was full of jelly, and Ben bent, undoing Fred's leash, biting back a smile when Stef winced as he traipsed across the white rug.

Sweetheart jumped up to kiss Fred's face, the pair of them circling each other before taking off, nails clicking on the floor.

Stef winced again.

"What?" he asked.

"He'll scratch your floor."

He snagged her purse from her, dropping it onto the table where he left his keys. Then he wove an arm around her waist and tugged her close, his other hand slipping into her hair, tilting her head back. "Baby," he said, "I'm only going to tell you this once." Her throat worked, and he ignored the temptation of that creamy skin, continuing, "Fred could chew up the couch cushions, could shit on this white rug. He could scratch the floor and dump over the garbage, and *I wouldn't care.*"

A breath shuddered out of her, coating his lips.

"Everything here is replaceable. It's all just stuff. He and you are more important."

A slow blink, her brown eyes chock full of emotions. "But you don't know me."

He trailed his fingers along that throat. "I know enough," he said. "And I know enough to know that what I'll learn won't change that fact."

She swallowed.

"Okay?"

Her nostrils flared on an inhale. Then they relaxed, her mouth curving into a small smile. "Okay."

"Friends, too?"

Her lips tipped up further. "We all usually have dinner on Thursday. If we're all in town," she added.

"Are you having dinner *this* Thursday?"

A nod.

"I'm coming."

"Okay," she said again.

"Okay." He brought her a little closer. "And now, I'm going to kiss you."

"It's about time."

Sweet and soft, a flash of fire and spice . . . and red, *red* lips. *God*, he liked this woman.

He dropped his head, took her mouth in a kiss that he felt to his toes, that rebuilt him from the bottom up to the top, cell by cell by cell.

Now, he just needed to do the same for her.

———

NAILS CLICKING on the floor had broken their kiss.

Or rather, their make out session, as their kiss had transitioned from standing in the middle of that rug to the table where he dropped his keys. He'd set her on top, stepped between her thighs, and let their tongues dance together, all while mentally making a note to fuck her here as soon as possible.

Preferably without two dogs nudging at his knees.

Stef was out of breath and looking deliciously rumpled, her lips swollen, and her fingers clenched into the fabric of his shirt.

He wanted to kiss her again.

To not stop.

But Fred—now nudging harder at the back of his knee—was apparently hungry.

Reluctantly, he pulled his mouth away from Stef's and glanced down at the cute, fluffy cock-blocker. "You hungry?"

Fred's tongue lolled out of his mouth in a way that seemed to signal the affirmative. Smothering a smile, he helped Stef down from the table, made sure she was steady on her feet. Then he took her hand and led her into the kitchen.

"Come on, pups"—he slanted a glance to his red-lipped, curvy woman—"and Stef. It's time for dinner."

This time, her smile wasn't filled with any uncertainty.

This time, her smile didn't come after a moment of hesitation.

This time, she just met his eyes, gave him her unhindered smile, and asked, "What'd you cook me?"

CHAPTER TWENTY-FIVE

Stef

SHE WAS WAITING outside the restaurant, trying not to shiver against the chilly air, nerves bubbling up in her throat.

It was Thursday.

She and Ben hadn't spent a night apart since the previous Friday.

Tuesday he'd come to her place.

Wednesday she'd gone to his again.

Tonight she was going back to his place, had actually boarded Fred for the evening, not that he was sad about getting extra doggy day care time, and Ben had asked his assistant—no VP—Claire to watch Sweetheart for the night.

Because he wanted to take her somewhere after dinner.

Somewhere he wouldn't divulge.

But somewhere he'd said wasn't time dependent when she'd worried about the dinner running long and ruining his plans.

He'd merely nuzzled her throat, fingers threading through her hair, and had told her, "It'll hold if you're too tired or it gets late. Just have fun with your friends, and we'll see how it goes."

And her heart, already vulnerable from that first night nearly a week ago, from the dinner he'd cooked on Monday and brought for her on the other days, from the coffee and bagel and food for Fred, from the other small things he'd paid attention to, had firmly cracked open.

She was exposed.

She was gone for him.

As she'd known she would be three months before, when she'd avoided that coffee date.

As she'd known when he'd left on Sunday, and she'd convinced herself he wouldn't come back.

And Stef was scared.

So fucking happy and sexually sated and enjoying the hell out of Ben, but she was also scared of what would happen to her when it ended. Still *when*, no matter if he'd said he'd stick around. Because a week wasn't enough time for him to find what everyone else had, to know her, *all* of her, including the parts that made people leave.

So, she was scared for a lot of reasons—because he might—probably would—leave and then she would be broken, because he might not show up that evening or her friends might hate him or—

Knuckles down her cheek.

A soft kiss to her forehead. "I'm going to show you," he murmured against her skin, slipping an arm around her shoulders and tugging her close.

And that right there was another reason she was freaking terrified.

Because she wanted to believe him.

Was quite desperate to.

Was quite desperate to kiss him, since it had been nearly twelve hours since she'd last had her mouth to his and when he was kissing her, she could pretend that everything was fine and her world hadn't been tilted on an axis it might eventually topple off, all in a little less than a week.

He brushed his thumb over her bottom lip, and she shuddered, lifting on tiptoe, her hand on his chest and able to feel the thundering of his heart beneath.

His arm around her shoulders tightened. His mouth came close.

Her tongue darted out, wet her bottom lip, and—

"*Ahem.*"

Stef startled, nearly flying out of Ben's arms, but he merely tightened his grip, brushed his thumb over her mouth once more.

An impatient tap of a foot. "Well, are you going to introduce us?"

She stifled a groan, ignoring Ben as he chuckled before releasing her, turning them to face Heidi, who was standing hand in hand with Brad, the former's tone sharp, though seriously tempered by the utter delight and mischief on her face. Brad, on the other hand, was staring at them with curiosity.

"Heidi, meet Ben."

Heidi's eyes narrowed, and Stef couldn't resist interjecting a little bit of teasing. God knew she'd be getting plenty of it inside the restaurant and for the foreseeable future. It was the way of her friends, to give as good as they got, and since this was the first time Stef had dated anyone since Jeremy, she knew there was to be no little amount of playful banter. Most of it at her expense. "Ben, this is my boss and bully of a friend, Heidi, and her lovely husband, Brad."

Heidi gasped.

Cora, who was just walking up behind their friend, cackled, her brown curls bouncing. And God, she seriously had the *best* hair. "Hi, lovely Brad," she said, kissing him on his cheek. "And bullying Heidi." She came over to Stef and Ben, narrowing her eyes at the latter. "You will treat my girl like the queen she is."

Stef winced, opened her mouth to . . . say something.

But Ben merely nodded. "Yes, I will."

"Good."

A beat as he extended a hand, his other arm still around Stef's shoulders as he lightly rubbed his palm up and down her arm, knowing she was nervous and soothing her; be still her heart. "I'm Ben."

Her friend studied his arm then Stef's face, but after a moment, she shook Ben's hand. "Cora."

A breeze kicked up, and Stef shivered, burrowing into his warmth. He nudged her toward the door. "Why don't you head inside? I can wait here for everyone else."

It was silly, but they always waited outside for everyone before they sat down at their table. She didn't know who had started the tradition, but it was kind of nice, all walking in as a big group together. They always made a reservation, usually sat at the same table, but it was different chatting with everyone outside—no interruptions from the waiter taking orders or food or drinks being delivered. Just them and their little circle of small talk before everyone came and voices started getting lost, conversations flowing over one another.

"You don't know everyone else," she pointed out.

"I'm sure I can figure it out," he began, right as Jaime, Tammy, and Kate, along with Kels and Tanner walked up.

Introductions were made, small talk commenced, and though she was shivering through her hoodie, she was loving the anecdote Jaime was telling about a kitten he'd taken care of that day. Ben shifted, slipping his arm away, but a moment later, his jacket was around her shoulders, his arm on top, and she was wonderfully warm.

And surrounded in the masculine spice of him.

She glanced up at him, but his gaze was on Jaime, lips turned up.

As though sensing her look, he glanced down, brushed his mouth over her forehead, and then returned his focus to Jaime, who was getting to the punch line of the little mischief maker clawing her way up his arm to perch on his head . . . and then launch herself on top of the cabinets in the back of the office.

It had taken them nearly thirty minutes to get her down, mostly because she was yowling over her predicament, and all the staff couldn't stop laughing.

And neither could they, because Jaime was damned good at telling stories.

But eventually they got it together and moved into the restaurant, Ben holding the door for them as they moved inside.

Cora lingered at the tail-end of the group, pausing and studying Ben once more. Only this time, her eyes relaxed, and she rose on tiptoe to press a kiss to his cheek. "Thank you," she said softly before she moved inside.

Stef, trailing her friend, did the same, adding after her thanks, "She likes you."

Ben winked, ushered her inside.

And then they went to dinner.

———

"WHAT DO YOU DO?" Kate asked, as they sat around the table, beers and prickly pear margaritas in hand.

Stef's gut seized, remembering the way he'd reacted that first night.

But tonight, Ben was relaxed, his mouth soft and curved when he shrugged. "I'm the CEO at Hunt Inc."

There were raised brows all around, but Kate just smiled. "I loved the new movie. Did you have any part in that?"

He shook his head. "No. I just helped negotiate some of the distribution deal. Though I can't even take credit for that. I'm just lucky to have great people working for me."

"That's why you looked familiar," Kels said. "I read an article about you a couple of years ago. Didn't you build the initial streaming platform yourself?"

Ben nodded. "As clunky as it was, I did. Luckily, I was able to bring on some engineers much better than I to perfect it, and they did such a great job that we were able to transition into creating our own content." He chuckled. "I'm much better with contracts and ideas than the nitty-gritty of actual programming."

Kels turned to Tanner. "He's being modest. He actually revolutionized the delivery system. That's why Hunt Inc. got so many users. Instead of the menus being so clunky, he streamlined it and made it very user-friendly—"

"We know it's user-friendly," Cora drawled. "That's why we all use it."

Stef bit back a smile as she studied Ben's face, and she had the feeling that he was blushing. She squeezed his hand, opened her mouth to change the subject, but Kels kept talking.

"But how did you come up with that algorithm to suggest recommended content? It's a freaking stroke of genius."

"Um," Ben said.

Kels kept going. "No, really. You've got to tell me how you came up with the idea for the source code. It's so much better than—"

Tanner covered her mouth with his hand. "Nice to have you here, Ben."

Kels's eyes narrowed.

"Why don't we let the poor man off the hot seat?"

"Yes, please," Ben muttered.

"Seriously," Cora said. "My brain is bleeding."

Kate, nice as always, tried to turn the conversation to something else. "Tell me about work, Kels. Did you finish your project?"

Kels, the smartest one of them, was thankfully as excited enough about her latest project—something about improving the delivery system for one of RoboTech's newest drone systems—to get off the topic of Ben's algorithm she was lusting over.

Unfortunately, her project and subsequent explanation was just as dry.

Which meant that Heidi and Cora listened for about three seconds before pouncing on Stef.

"You owe me details," Heidi said. "You've been avoiding telling me how you met Ben all week."

She felt Ben look down at her, but she didn't glance up.

She *had* been avoiding telling the story.

Not because she was embarrassed, but because having a *How We Met* story felt like they had a relationship, and then having a relationship—or the possibility of one—had her heart clenching and worry creeping in and—

Ben squeezed her hand.

"I met her outside of Bobby's. We saw a movie and hit it off, and I've been trying to tempt her into spending as much time with me as possible."

Cora grinned.

Heidi studied him closely. "Why do I feel like there's more to the story?"

Because there was.

But she wasn't going to share her breakdown three months before, nor the fact that she'd drunk messaged him on Tinder, nor that they'd only been seeing each other for a week.

It felt longer, and she supposed it was in a way.

In the past, when she had gone on a date with someone, she'd seen them once a week, maybe a couple times a month. Then they parted ways or moved up to twice a week.

She and Ben were on date . . . seven? Maybe eight or nine if she counted the full day on Saturday and Sunday as separate from the evenings.

Yes, she was grasping at straws.

Yes, it made her feel better to think that their time together was equivalent to two months of dating.

"Whatcha thinking?" Ben murmured.

She blinked, realized that Heidi had gotten pulled into conversation with Kate, Cora with Tammy, and Ben was staring down at her quizzically.

And his eyes were so pretty that she found herself blurting, "I was adding up our dates."

He lifted a brow.

"We've had two months' worth, in case you were wondering."

His lips quirked. "Yeah?"

She nodded, grinning at her own silliness. "Yeah."

He lifted her hand, pressed a kiss to the back of it. "Well, that sounds like a good start."

The server came with their food then, but the words were pinging around her brain. Simple words, but they unlocked something inside her. Because it *was* a start, and even if it would have an end, if she spent all her time being focused on it, then she was missing out on the now.

Missing out on the good times they were having.

Not that she was doing it every moment, but she was spending enough time worrying about it to pull her away from Ben, from her friends, from the fun and loveliness of *now*.

She dropped her hand to his thigh, leaned up to kiss his cheek.

He turned his head, eyes blazing.

"A good start," she agreed.

Those knuckles found her throat, brushing lightly over her skin. "Eat, honey. Put those Hoovering skills to work."

Her heart kicked against her ribs, love blossomed somewhere deep inside her.

But she didn't panic.

Instead, she embraced the feeling . . . and got down to eating her fajitas.

CHAPTER TWENTY-SIX

Ben

STEF SMELLED like heaven as she leaned against him, riding the elevator all the way to the top of the Hunt Inc. building.

The reason he hadn't been worried about how long dinner would take.

He'd just wanted to bring her here.

To show her this.

The elevator doors opened into a dim hallway, and she slowed, lifting an eyebrow. "Um, so you don't have a creepy serial killer basement, but you have a creepy, dark hallway instead?"

He tugged a lock of her hair. "Just a short one."

"That's what she said."

He burst out laughing, shook his head, and stepped ahead of her to push open the door at the end of it.

"Oh," she murmured.

And he knew the feeling. It was the same one that he'd had when he'd first come up here after he'd bought the building.

Now it had been spruced up.

A safety railing added, several couches on one side, a table between them. Even an outdoor heater.

But the suave furnishings weren't what he wanted to show her.

Instead, it was the view.

"Wow," she said, when he'd taken her hand and coaxed her out. She still wore his jacket, hadn't taken it off since he'd settled it on her shoulders. "This is amazing."

He brought her to the railing, to the view that had taken his breath from the first moment he'd seen it. The lights of San Francisco glowed in the distance, some twinkling and bright, others more muted by the curls of fog coming in from the ocean. The Golden Gate was to the north, the lights of the East Bay visible on the other side of the inlet of water.

"I grew up there," he said softly.

Stef turned from where she'd been looking at the Golden Gate and curled into his side. "Across the Bay?"

He nodded. "In Hayward."

"I haven't heard of it."

He tugged a lock of her hair. "I forget that you didn't grow up here. It's a smaller city between San Jose and Oakland. Great place when I was a kid, but it changed when I got older."

"In what way?"

"Got bigger, felt less like that small town, and . . ." The words got stuck in his throat, but she just waited for him to find his voice again. "It was still home. I loved the hills and the downtown. We had a special curb."

Her head tilted to the side as she glanced up at him with questions in her eyes. "A curb?"

He flashed a smile. "Yup."

"C-u-r-b? As in one you stepped off." Her brows drew together. "I'm struggling to understand the significance."

Laughter flowed up his throat, filled the air around them. "It was built on a fault line, so every year it moved, separating from the sidewalk, jutting out a little more." He shrugged. "It was always cool to go see it and measure it, to see how many millimeters it moved from one year to the next. A stupid thing, but my mom and I would keep track of our measurements in a notebook. We'd be so freaking careful to make sure we took them in the same exact spot. And my dad would be sitting on a bench across the street, a stack of books from the library in his arms, reading through one as we fussed."

"That sounds really nice."

"It was." A beat. "Until they fixed the curb, and we couldn't measure anymore."

Stef gasped. "They didn't."

"Unfortunately, they did. I guess the city thought it was getting dangerous." Another shrug. "And I supposed that I thought I was getting too old to enjoy doing it anyway. A teenager who was too cool to hang with his parents."

"I'm sorry."

"Because I was a pain in the ass teenager?"

She pinched his hip. "No," she said. "But because you lost that part of your past."

He'd never thought about it that way.

But he supposed he'd been mourning for it in some small way since his mom had passed, missing all the easy times of the traditions they'd had, the chance to make new memories with her.

"What happened to your parents?" she asked gently. "You said they were gone, but . . ."

He blinked, and for a moment, grief threatened to swell up over him, but he battled it back, kept this woman who had become intrinsic to his life in such a short time close. "My mom died a year ago, my dad five years before that."

"I'm sorry."

"What about yours?" He slid his hand up and down her arm.

"They still live in the town I grew up in." There was a note of sadness in her tone, and he wondered if he should ask about it, but then she kept talking. "Still the same house, actually. Hell, they drove the same station wagon from my teenage years until two years ago when it broke down and the mechanic couldn't find parts to repair it." The words came fast and furious. "So, they were stuck buying a new car and hated every minute of it." Her voice had been overcome with sadness, the words finally coming to a halt.

"You want to talk about it?" he asked after she'd gone quiet and stayed that way for several moments.

She cleared her throat. "No," she whispered. "I'm sorry I hijacked your story."

He frowned. "I asked you about your family."

"Right." Another whisper, something fragile in her tone.

"I want to know all the things that make you tick."

A shudder wracked her frame, and this time it wasn't from the cold or the way he was holding her, touching her. This was a pain remembered, slices of agony that ran deep inside a person's soul. He knew because like recognized like, because he'd so often felt those same cuts after his father had been murdered, after cancer had stolen his mother. Two good people taken, leaving him behind with just memories. So, he stayed quiet, held her close, and waited.

"You don't."

He opened his mouth to argue, but then she was pulling out of his hold and moving over to the railing, hands gripping on the metal bar. He might have let her have the moment, allowed the quiet to grow and stay that way if not for her wiping away a tear.

Just a sly small motion, fingers darting up for her eye.

But he *did* see it.

And he was moving toward her before he even registered that his feet were in motion.

"Hey," he said softly. "What is it?"

She shook her head, wouldn't look at him. "I'm sorry."

Another apology.

"Stef." He turned her to him, hooked a finger under her chin. "Honey, *what is it?*"

She stepped away from him, tears glistening on her cheeks. "I'm so—"

"Don't apologize," he snapped, not as gently as it should have been, worry having crept in as the tears started to come in full force. "Tell me what's wrong."

But she either couldn't or wouldn't, and when she stumbled back a pace and bent at the waist, a sob hiccupping out of her lungs, he closed the distance between them, scooped her up and carried her to the couch.

And all the while she kept apologizing.

And all the while he kept telling her to *stop* apologizing.

But eventually, he realized that his orders weren't helping anything and just shut up and held her as she cried, as she repeated, "I'm sorry. I'm sorry," over and over again.

It killed him, that painful nonstop rhetoric, as though by saying it repeatedly she was atoning for something.

What could she possibly have to atone for?

He knew he needed to find out, that it was locked up with whatever he'd seen the previous Sunday, what had occasionally crept into her eyes throughout the week—the expectation that he would look too close and then leave.

This was the puzzle piece to the distance she held.

The wall she'd erected, the barb that was shoving them apart.

When all he wanted was to get closer.

Finally, she grew quiet and limp in his arms, and he was almost afraid to speak, afraid that if he gave voice to any of the thoughts in his head, she would retreat. So he held his tongue, stared out at the lights, and just stroked a hand up and down her spine.

The words, when they eventually came, surprised him.

Because he didn't talk about it.

Hadn't *ever* talked about it.

Not with his mother. Not with Claire or Baine, who'd been with him when he'd received the phone call.

He'd buried it down. Deep down. Perhaps as deeply as this pain of Stef's was buried.

"My father isn't just gone," he said. "He was murdered."

Stef's breathing had slowed, but when he spoke, it picked up again.

"He was just driving home from work," Ben said. "Stopped at a signal, and someone shot him through the window, yanked him out of his car with a bullet wound to the chest, and drove off." Ben's gaze turned to the Bay Bridge, to the steady stream of red and white lights from cars that made their way back and forth across the bottom and top decks—away from the city on the bottom, to it on the top. "They left him to die in the middle of the street and then took his car."

"Oh, Ben," she whispered. "I'm so sorry."

"The police found it three blocks away, parked half up on the curb, the door wide open. They took it and just *left* it there, discarded it like they had no use for it, for him—" His voice cracked.

She shifted in his arms, her hand lifting to rest on his jaw. "I'm sorry," she said again.

He covered the back of her palm with his own. "I miss him. Every day, I miss him."

Another tear slid down her cheek. "I know, baby."

He lifted his hand to wipe it away, and she shifted, wrapped her arms around his waist, nuzzling into his throat.

"I miss him, too," she said, so softly that he could hardly discern the words. "I shouldn't miss him so much. I'm not worthy of that grief, not when part of me hated him so much when he was alive."

Ben's heart ached at the agony of her words, but part of him also hoped.

Hoped so fucking much that she would share her hurt with him, allow him to take some of it away.

Instead, she held on tight to him, and he stayed quiet.

For minutes.

For hours.

Until the moon began to set, and Stef's breathing went slow and steady, and he knew she'd fallen asleep in his arms.

Not tonight then.

Ben grasped on to his patience, held it firm, and carried her downstairs to his car, drove her back to his place.

Soon. He had to hope that soon she would give him the rest.

Because he'd take it, would wrap it up carefully inside him, remove the hurt, the agony, and he would give her back happy.

He would do anything to give her back happy.

CHAPTER TWENTY-SEVEN

Stef

STEF WOKE up and instantly knew where she was.

In Ben's arms.

In Ben's bed.

And even though exhaustion still tugged at her, she smiled. Because she really liked waking up with him.

As though sensing that she was awake, his eyes opened and his face gentled. "Morning, baby."

"Morning," she whispered, wanting to brush her fingers over his jaw.

As though sensing *that*, he tipped his head down, close enough so that his forehead rested against hers, so that she could easily touch him.

"You okay?" His eyes were on hers.

She nodded.

Then noticed the time on the clock on his nightstand. "Shit! I'm late." She started to toss the blankets back, to slide out of bed, but Ben merely clamped a hand around her arm and tugged her back against him, rolling to pin her between him and the mattress.

Hard lines. Hard muscles. Hard . . . cock.

She shivered.

He grinned.

And suddenly, work became the last thing on her mind.

"I called Heidi last night," he murmured. "Told her you wouldn't be in today." Her mouth dropped open. "Same as I called Claire and told her to forget my phone number for the day."

Stef's eyes widened.

"And she's going to keep Sweetheart. And doggy day care is going to keep Fred for one more night."

"I—"

His hips dropped down onto hers. "Is that okay?"

Her lips parted, her breathing shaky as pleasure began coiling itself like a snake in her abdomen. Always like this. Always needing him so fiercely.

"Baby?"

Heidi was probably going to interrogate her to no end, and she'd be hopelessly behind on Monday, but, "Yes, it's okay." It was wonderful actually. She hadn't taken a day off in ages, not one during the week anyway, ignoring her responsibilities for the day. She didn't think that she'd ever played hooky, nor had anyone she'd dated gone so far for her.

To call in to her boss.

To take care of her dog.

To think about the details so she didn't have to.

Falling. Falling. So fucking deep, and . . . she couldn't bring herself to care, couldn't do anything except push back against his chest.

He moved instantly, giving her distance.

But it wasn't distance that she wanted. Instead, she kept pushing, rolling him onto his back, clambering on top of him. Hands perched on his pecs, massaging the muscles that over-filled her hands, dragging her nails over his nipples, loving the hiss of his breath escaping the mouth she was suddenly quite desperate to kiss.

So, she did.

And had the lovely side benefit of being pressed to every inch of him, of tasting him, of his slightly roughened fingers coming to her ass.

She'd made a tactical error in not getting naked first.

Otherwise, she would have those hands on her bare skin.

Ben's moan rumbled up his throat, filling her mouth, drifting down along her spine, winding its way between her legs. Her underwear was sopping wet, the T-shirt—Ben's, she now realized—a cumbersome hindrance when she wanted her skin against his.

Forcing herself to break the kiss, she reared back and yanked off the material, thankful that Ben was reaching for her hips, shoving her panties down her thighs, not bothering to propel them farther than her knees. Which was fine with her because then his fingers slid back up and in between, stroking through the evidence of her desire. So wet. Always so wet for him.

She went to work on his boxer briefs, pushing the material out of her way, revealing the hard cock encased within.

"Yes," she breathed, wrapping her hand around him and pumping.

Velvet over scorching steel.

He circled her clit, dipped a finger down and in, making her arch back against him, riding his hand as pleasure rocketed through her.

So quickly, she was close already.

But she didn't want to come.

Or at least, she didn't want to come *yet*.

She wanted him *in* and deep and thrusting hard and fast.

Shifting, she dislodged his fingers, started to ease down on him, the broad, bare head of his cock stretching her wide.

"Wait," he murmured, reaching a hand overhead for the nightstand. "Condom."

All the movement did was push him deeper inside her, making them both groan. "I have an IUD. Are you clean?"

"Yes." He groaned. "Just had a physical last week."

"Thank God," she said. "I'm clean, too. Was tested after my ex and I . . ." Her hips weren't in her control, not in the least, rocking and shifting, bringing him deeper and deeper, and though it felt so fucking good, she paused, met his gaze. "I haven't been with anyone else. I want you without—" She broke off, nibbled at her bottom lip.

"Yes," he panted, his fingers clutching her hips.

"Yes," she repeated. Then, "Come inside me?"

He bucked, impaling himself deep, and they both groaned again, louder this time, and hers might have been a scream, but she didn't care. Not when his hands were gripping her tightly, bringing her down on top of him, over and over again.

Not when his abs flexed, curling his shoulders up, changing the angles of their bodies so he could hit just the right spot.

"Fuck," he growled. "You are so fucking beautiful."

He was the beautiful one, or the things they were doing, building were beautiful, or . . . maybe she was beautiful. At least, the person she could dream about becoming. That confident, gorgeous woman was there, just within reach if only—

Ben's thumb moved between them, pressing against her clit, just the way she liked.

Thoughts of beauty faded into thoughts of need, of desperation.

She moved faster, driving herself down onto his cock, her orgasm barreling toward her with the force of a hurricane, swirling and whipping her around and around, bearing down on her, and—

Boom.

The force of it rattled her to her core, pleasure condensing and then flaring out, forcing her to move faster and faster and *faster* until the waves of that bliss eddied, until Ben was gripping her tight and pouring himself inside her as he came.

She collapsed.

His arms wrapped around her.

She buried her face in his throat, inhaled the scent of him deep inside her.

And because they were playing hooky, she let sleep drag her back under.

———

FOUR WEEKS LATER, she was still in the same blissful cloud.

She and Ben had spent that day playing hooky in bed together, making love until they were too exhausted to do anything but order in food and sleep and watch old Sci-Fi shows on TV.

They'd laughed and cuddled before doing it all again.

Sex. Talk about work. About movies and TV and pop culture.

Ben had told her about his parents, about building his company, and how he'd started developing the idea for Hunt Inc., how it had started as something small that could be an alternative to the big streaming networks, then had developed into something much bigger than he could have anticipated.

And now was their major competitor.

He was busy, very busy with meetings all day.

They didn't talk or text during those hours, which was just as well, since her phone needed to remain off most of the time, but he had recently introduced a hard stop at six, no matter what was happening, and he expected it to be the same for everyone beneath him. No emails. No calls.

Just people able to go about their lives without work's shadow constantly intruding. Easier to see how important that was now that he actually *had* a life.

Untraditional, same as the remote work he allowed his staff to do without question or clearance.

But it made for happy employees.

Plus, she got him all evening with no interruptions. Which was more than she could say for herself. Sometimes she had to be on call for the lab, if an experiment was running overnight or throughout a weekend, and if there was an issue, she had to go in.

They'd gone out every Thursday with her friends, and tonight—*tonight!*—she was meeting his friends.

Claire, Baine, and Spence. Oh, along with CJ, because Ben's newest assistant, was coming along, too. Apparently, Spence was a little quiet but a nice guy, and they were trying to get him to hang out more. CJ would likely be freaked out and silent, but Ben was convinced it was important for them all to hang out. And Stef agreed. A work environment where everyone was comfortable with each other was better for everyone.

Claire and Baine, on the other hand, had been with him from nearly the beginning and were chomping at the bit—Claire, especially, according to Ben—to meet her. *Meet* might be code for interrogating her, but he'd been interrogated plenty by her friends, so she figured he was due.

But, as she surveyed her closet, what did one wear to a future interrogation?

A dress? Jeans and a T-shirt?

Something in between?

In the end, she decided on jeans, a blouse, and knee-high boots, a simple infinity scarf around her neck to ward off the night air.

So, maybe she was a basic bitch.

And she didn't give a damn. They would pry her skinny jeans and scarves off her cold, dead body.

"Exactly," she muttered as she finished slicking on her lipstick, of which she'd had to buy extra tubes because Ben kissed it off her so often. Not that he seemed to mind his own lips getting stained from her, and she loved the gleam that came into his eyes when he wiped his mouth of the lipstick.

The wicked glint.

The promise of more.

More.

She was starting to believe that *more* was a possibility. She'd certainly had more with Ben than she'd ever had with anyone else. They fit, and she liked the person she was with him, especially since she'd stopped doubting every gesture and promise.

He showed up when he said he would. He called or texted to check in with her during the rare times they were apart, and he wasn't passive-aggressive. He meant what he said, and there was no hidden message she needed to untangle. And beyond that, he was . . . nice and patient. He made her smile.

She was happier than she'd been in ages. Maybe ever.

Five weeks they'd had.

And he hadn't turned away from her, hadn't pushed her to share things that made her sad, not because he didn't notice when something made her sad, but because he did. He'd ask if she wanted to share, and when she'd found the words stoppered up, unable to admit that final piece of her that she held back, he'd just held or kissed her, murmured again that he would show her.

Five times seven was thirty-five. Plus eight for the four weekends together. Forty-three days. How many months of dating was that?

Six? Seven?

Enough that she was thinking about it.

Enough that she *wanted* to tell him, because he'd shown her repeatedly that he was patient and kind.

Enough that she desired to let go of the burden.

This weekend.

She'd do it this weekend.

CHAPTER TWENTY-EIGHT

Ben

CLAIRE LEANED back in her chair, hazel eyes sparkling, curly brown hair shining under the lights as Stef burst into laughter.

He wanted to close the distance between them, to kiss the woman he was utterly in love with—Stef, not Claire—though he loved the latter, too, albeit in a sisterly fashion, and despite her efforts to embarrass him.

"And then he came to that first production meeting with his hair all messed up, his shirt half-unbuttoned, and smelling like booze."

Baine gave him a wolfish smile. Spence looked vaguely uncomfortable, having said only a handful of words. CJ had been still and silent as a statue.

"In fairness for my idiocy," Ben said. "I'd never been to a strip club, and that one"—he pointed at Baine—"decided that I *needed* to have the full experience."

"You were twenty-seven and hadn't had a lap dance. That needed to be remedied."

Stef's grin stayed in place, but Ben saw a glimmer of insecurity dancing on the edges of her expression.

Baine got that, too, and he didn't lie to her, just said the words that would put her at ease. "This one hated it. Sat there like a statue when I brought the girls over, no matter how many drinks I bought him."

The insecurity faded. "Not your thing?"

Ben shook his head, but Baine answered for him. "Definitely not his thing. No matter how much I coaxed, I couldn't get him back there."

"It was too much for this nerd," Ben said lightly. "Plus, I had enough people trying to get close to me because of Hunt. I didn't need an entire club's worth doing that."

Baine shrugged. "At least you knew what they were after the moment you walked through the door."

He considered that, nodded. "That's true," he agreed.

"But still not your thing," Stef murmured.

Lacing his fingers with hers, he brought them up to his mouth and kissed them lightly. "For the scrawny kid who didn't even have a date to prom . . . it was less a fantasy and more a nightmare."

Claire tsked. "Oh poor, poor CEO. Everyone wants a piece of him."

Baine snorted.

Ben rolled his eyes.

Spence's cheeks went a little pink. CJ still played statue.

Stef bristled, turning to Claire, her delicate features pulled into a scowl. "He's allowed to feel the way he feels," she ground out, adding when Claire scoffed, "And those feelings are valid, whether or not you think they are."

A glimpse of the fire beneath the sweet.

Hidden steel wielded for him.

Claire leaned forward. "You have a defender."

Stef narrowed her eyes. "Ben is a good man, and he deserves your respect. He's done so much for me and—"

Silence.

Then Claire's voice took on a note of cold, one that drew Ben's sharp glare. "And what has he done, exactly?"

He could read the undertones in the question, same as Stef could, if her going stiff as a board beside him was any indication. "Claire," he began, warning lacing his tone.

Stef talked over him. "He's given me hope."

More silence.

She spoke softly but fiercely, each word carefully clipped out. "And shown me that I can trust people again. Not because I was dragged along by someone else, included because someone took pity on me and brought me along. Not even because he's stuck with me due to us working together, like . . ." Her lips pressed flat then relaxed, voice even softer, and he realized she was talking about her friends, about Heidi. "Ben chose me, and I know what a gift that is."

His heart thudded, twisting the words over in his mind.

She thought her friends only liked her because of some bizarre obligation?

That drove a blade right through his insides. He wanted to yank her out of this restaurant, find some quiet place, and yell at her until she realized that she was loveable and worthy of her friends. Then he wanted to track down Jeremy Whatever-His-Name was and hurt him for hurting her. *Then* he wanted to find out who else had hurt her because he understood now that her wounds weren't from one man. They ran deeper than that, ingrained so deeply that they'd been imprinted on her soul.

"And you've known him how long? A month—"

Ben jerked his gaze to Claire. "That's—"

"Yes," Stef snapped. "A month. Or five weeks, if we're not counting that we first talked four months ago and that I chickened out and ended it." She rolled her shoulders, and he hated the glimmer of disgust on her face, but she kept talking before he could take her to task for it. "Try as I might, I couldn't get him out of my mind, and found that I had to talk to him, so I reached out, and we've been together since. So yeah, maybe we've been dating for barely more than a month, and maybe that's not a long time, but maybe it *doesn't* always take a long time." She inhaled, released it slowly, her tone gentling. "Life can change in a minute, an hour. Life can change the moment that you meet someone. Life doesn't follow a set of rules, and when you find someone who's worth you taking a fucking risk, you grab on tight."

Ben was too stunned, too touched by her words to manage to do anything other than just stare at her in awe.

Her color was high.

Her eyes flashed with temper.

But her grip on his hand was gentle.

"For the record," she continued, Claire having fallen silent, Baine, CJ, and Spence no doubt gaping very much like he was.

She had a heart of fire, a spine of steel, and had unleashed that for him.

For *him.*

"Ben was that for me."

She turned, her gaze alighting on his, something warring within her gaze, as though she were trying to come to terms with a decision. Then she seemed to come to it, straightening her shoulders and saying softly, "I love you."

Electricity shot down his spine.

But before he could recover, she stood. "Excuse me. I need to use the restroom."

Then she took off across the restaurant, disappearing down the hall, and moving out of sight.

"I like her," Claire breathed.

Baine grunted in agreement.

CJ and Spence didn't say anything.

But Ben barely noticed. He was already on his feet, following her.

———

BUT SHE WASN'T in the bathroom.

Wasn't in either of the two single stalls—a fact he knew because he'd actually checked in both, barging in front of a couple of people waiting and peering inside.

She definitely hadn't come out of the hall, so the only logical place she could have disappeared through was the back door. He moved swiftly to it, pushing the steel panel wide and searching the dimly lit alley behind the restaurant.

Nothing.

Nothing.

There.

He moved to her. "Stef."

She turned, blinked up at him, tears clinging to her lashes. "I'm sorry," she said. "Your friends—"

"Are as in love with you as I am," he interrupted swiftly. "Claire, especially, as it takes a rare person to both laugh at her stories and to shut her down when she goes too far."

"I'm—"

"Stef, baby," he said, tugging her against him. "I love you, but I swear to God, if you apologize one more time, I will not be held accountable for my actions."

A chuckle bubbled up in the space between them. "Are those supposed to be sweet words?"

"No," he said, and was relieved to see light enter her eyes. "But these are." Lightly, he brushed back her hair, brushed a kiss over her forehead. "I look at your face and I'm stunned by your beauty, but the way you look here"—he ran a finger over her lips, her jaw, one eyebrow and then the other—"is nothing compared to the woman in *here*." He placed a hand over her heart. "I've spent every night with you because I can't stay away, because the moment I began talking to you, I felt like I was home again, like the sun was shining down on me, the clouds having finally, *finally* cleared."

"Ben," she whispered.

"I saw red lips and curves, was desperate to taste them both, but when I talked to you, when I held you, I knew a taste would never be enough. I want to spend an eternity with you, every night from now until they put me in the ground."

A tear slid from her eye, and he brushed it away. "Ben," she whispered again.

He loved the sound of his name on her tongue, hated the sight of her tears, even though these were of happiness. "Should I keep going?"

She laughed as he brushed more tears away, the joy in her stare taking his breath away. "God no, I can't take it without turning into a complete watering pot."

"All right," he teased. "I'll save them for when we're in bed together."

Her red lips twitched. "Okay."

"Okay," he repeated, sliding his hand up and down her back, not wanting to let her go, but knowing they couldn't stand in this alley all night.

Stef seemed equally as reluctant, her arms wrapping around his waist, her breathing slow and deep. But eventually, she must have realized the same thing as him, "We should go inside," she said. "We're probably messing up their dinner."

Honestly, he didn't give a shit about Claire, Spence, CJ, and Baine's dinners.

He had the woman he loved in his arms, and she'd taken a huge step today. She'd been vulnerable and still let him in, trusted her with his heart. Ben knew exactly how big of a gift that was.

Because of that he didn't release her, not yet anyway. Instead, he wove his fingers into her hair and tilted her head back so that he could see her face. "Only if you do one thing for me."

She lifted her brows.

"No more apologies."

Those brows dragged together.

"You apologize too much for things that aren't your fault."

"I'm—"

"Uh-uh," he said, bopping her on the nose. "No sorries."

"I wasn't going to apologize," she huffed. "I was just going to say that I'm so glad you came back that day. That you're here in my life and—"

They needed to go inside.

But fuck if he could stop himself from kissing her again.

CHAPTER TWENTY-NINE

Stef

COME MONDAY, she still hadn't told Ben about Chance, about her parents and the twisted turn her childhood had taken.

Not because she was avoiding it.

But because Ben had kept her so busy in bed and at the beach and then watching an early release for a new movie Hunt was releasing. It was top secret, but he'd told her about it the week before. It featured a couple of Hollywood A-listers Stef loved, and he'd told her he'd had to beg, borrow, and practically steal the copy, just so he could bring the DVD home so she could see it. Despite the challenge, he'd brought it all the same, and she'd coaxed him into watching it twice (and crying both times).

And did she mention he'd kept her busy in bed? Because he'd been absolutely ravenous. Not that she hadn't been—*wasn't*—the same, needing him with an intensity that was all-consuming.

She was.

She looked at him, saw his smile, and she was wet.

Desire and orgasms aside, she'd decided that today would be the day. Her past was heavy. It was stifling. Not the topic for normal dinner time conversation. But she found that she needed to let that burden go.

Finally, she needed to be done with it.

So, she'd explain, tell him about her parents and Chance, about how she'd searched for her worth and value in other places.

And how she had finally begun to accept that her value came first from her.

Because Ben had given her the patience and kindness to understand that. By him seeing her value, loving her for being herself and not the over-the-top caregiver she'd been with Jeremy; nor the small, quiet, trying to never step a toe out of line girl she'd been with her parents; not even the everything was fine young woman she'd been with her college boyfriends and afterward, she found that worth.

She was done with always doing things for everyone but herself.

Done with thinking that doing something for herself, or wanting something, or saying no would be selfish when everyone else needed it more.

Because it was different with Ben.

He took care of her, making sure to give back what she offered freely . . . and that had opened doors inside her heart she had never risked cracking before, doors that had been slammed and locked for many years. He made her understand that a relationship could be different, that they could have give and take. It wasn't always perfectly equal, sometimes one person gave or took more, but when everything was averaged, their relationship wasn't lopsided.

Because he never took more than his fair share. In fact, if she were being truthful, she would say that he'd given more.

Tonight, however, would be different.

It was her turn to give more.

Smiling, she took the exit. She was heading back to her place after work, Fred in the back seat. She'd filled the Crock-Pot that morning with the one recipe for dinner that she couldn't fuck up, and she was going to feed the man, give him a glorious orgasm, and then pass over the final pieces of her, offer them up on a silver platter.

And she was going to hope that he didn't dump them on the floor.

Her stomach twisted, worry sliding through her.

"No," she gritted, gripping the steering wheel. "He's not going to do that. He's a good man and—*Ugh,* Fred!"

Her pup had licked her ear and she cringed, trying to drive as she wiped it on her shoulder, and not having much success. Luckily, she was almost home, just turning onto her street, so she just waited until she was in her driveway and parked to get the doggy saliva out of her ear.

"Thanks a lot, Fred," she muttered, shuddering as she dried her ear then reached for her purse. She got out, let Fred out, not bothering with the leash since he was sure to be focused on dinner and not on any rogue squirrels who might be lurking. He barked, and she kept muttering, grabbing a grocery bag with some prepacked salad and store-bought chocolate cake, "Hold your horses, bud. I'll be right . . . there?"

Finishing on a question came from the fact that the front door was open, and Fred had let himself inside.

She smiled, hurrying to the porch, thinking that Ben had beaten her here, and since she'd given him a key a couple of weeks before, he'd let himself in, too. Fred was probably excited to see him, and—

Another bark.

This one deeper. Not a friendly one.

Her eyes flicked to the driveway, to the street, across it, realizing that she didn't see Ben's car anywhere.

Fred barked again and then she heard a sharp, "Shut up!"

And then . . . a yelp.

She ran inside.

As stupid as it was, she ran inside her house. Because Fred had yelped, and she couldn't leave him to be hurt and . . .

She dropped her purse on the entryway floor when she saw who was there.

Jeremy. Rifling through the drawers in her kitchen.

Fred had backed himself into the corner, his teeth bared, and he seemed to be favoring one leg awkwardly.

And Stef saw red.

"What in the absolute fuck are you doing here?"

Jeremy stopped, turned to face her. "Where is it?"

She stifled a sigh. Were they really on this merry-go-round again?

"How did you get into my house?" she asked, carefully moving so that she put herself between Jeremy and Fred.

"*Where is it?!*" Jeremy screamed.

He looked unhinged, dark circles beneath his eyes, his cheekbones sharply pushing against pale, clammy skin, the stubble on his jaw patchy and overgrown.

Fear clamped a heavy hand on her shoulder.

He might hurt her, she suddenly realized. He might actually be capable of physically *hurting* her.

She'd never seriously considered that possibility before.

The truth had her pulse speeding until it was a rapid drum against her veins, her vision hazed and narrowed to the man who returned to searching through drawers, yanking one open and then the next, rifling through them, dropping the contents on the floor. She reached in her pocket for her cell, unlocked it as she asked, "Where is what, Jeremy?"

Another drawer's contents hit the floor, this one with silver-ware. It clattered deafeningly, forks and knives and spoons scattering in all directions. "You know," he muttered, moving to the next, dumping her towels out of it and yanking another open, nearly ripping it from its slides. "You damn well know."

Something snapped inside her. *"I don't know what the fuck you're talking about!"*

It was a mistake, that.

She'd snagged her phone, but hadn't unlocked it, hadn't dialed 9-1-1, or just grabbed Fred and got out. Then she'd yelled, loud enough to gain Jeremy's unhinged focus.

His *deadly* focus, if the gleam in his eyes was any indication.

He moved toward her, kicking his way across her belongings—a spatula going one way, several forks another, her turkey baster bouncing off the toe kick of the cabinets and skittering across the floor.

And he didn't stop moving, not even as he closed the distance between them, as Fred growled, as he grabbed her arm, yanked her to the side, and pinned her against the wall so quickly that her ankle exploded with pain. "Where." His fingers dug in hard enough to make her cry out in pain, her hand spasming, and her cell phone falling to the floor. "Is *it?*"

"I don't know—"

She didn't finish the rest of the statement because as suddenly as he'd cornered her, he was gone.

Just ripped away like the wind stealing a hat on a gusty day.

Ben gripped Jeremy by the throat, his face in a rage that was far scarier than Jeremy's, something that any sane person would see.

But Jeremy wasn't in his right mind.

He was gone to the anger, struggling against Ben's hold, even as Ben leveled a left hook at his face.

The sound was . . . gross. A crunching noise, blood immediately bursting from Jeremy's nose. It dripped down his chin, stained the front of his shirt, then more blood as Ben wound up and punched him again.

And again.

And again.

Until Jeremy was limp in his hold, his legs barely holding

him up, Ben's hand around his throat the single thing keeping him up.

"Get the fuck out of this house," Ben growled, propelling him to the front door, as though he weighed nothing. "And if I ever see you within fifty feet of Stef, I will cheerfully murder you and then pay someone to make sure your body is never found."

Jeremy sneered, his eyes rolling around in his head. "I—"

Ben shook him. "Am not going to say another word." A beat. "Because that would be the first good decision you've made since you decided to break up with Stef."

"She—"

Ben shook him again. "Is a fucking goddess who is too good for me and you?" A feral smile curved his lips. "You're right. She is. But your idiotic loss is my gain, and I will protect what is mine. So heed my words, *do not come back here.*"

Then he threw him out the front door, slammed it shut, and locked it.

Stef's knees gave way, and she found herself sliding down the wall, collapsing onto the floor. Tears leaked from her eyes, but she angrily brushed them away, turning her focus to Fred, even as her ankle screamed out in pain as she crawled toward him. Fred whined, his tail thwapping once on the floor. He tried to get up, but one of his back legs wouldn't work, so she held him in place. "No, buddy," she said through her tears, "just stay down."

She kept her hands on his side, scrabbled for her cell.

"Here," Ben said, handing it to her. "Are you all—"

Banging began on the front door, the wood panel rattling on its hinges, Jeremy screaming and ranting. Ben cursed, rising to his feet, at the same time sirens sounded, came close, and tires screeching somewhere close.

Perhaps her driveway.

Voices rose and fell, Jeremy's and several unfamiliar ones shouting orders. Jeremy refusing them.

Then a scuffling, a crash, more scuffling, and . . . finally, all went quiet.

Ben crossed to the door, but before he got there, a knock sounded through the panel.

She turned her head, watched as Ben carefully opened the door, keeping his hands open and wide at his side as police officers stood in the opening. "Thank you for coming," he said.

They studied him then her on the floor, Fred trying to get up.

"Are you okay, ma'am?"

She nodded. "Ben"—she pointed, wanting to be sure that they knew exactly who the good guy was—"is my boyfriend. He saved me from"—she nodded to the porch where her ex was trussed up like a turkey—"Jeremy. My ex who broke in and assaulted me. H-he—"

Then Ben was there at her side, pulling her into his arms. "It's okay. I'm here, baby. I'm here."

She clung to him. "Fred's hurt."

"I know." He pulled out his phone, spoke quickly into it. "Claire and Baine are coming. They'll get him to the vet."

"O-okay," she whispered, slipping out of his arms and turning back to her dog.

"Sir?" one of the officers asked. "Can we have a word?"

Ben gently cupped her cheek. "You okay for a minute?"

She nodded.

"Tell me what happened," she heard the officer said. "And start from the beginning."

"I pulled up and saw the front door was open," Ben began.

Fred whined, and she knew she should splint his leg, should do something useful, do something to make him more comfortable. Maybe get a towel under him so he would be easier to carry. She pushed her hands beneath herself, started to push to her feet.

She cried out and collapsed before she got there.

Instantly, Ben was there, two police officers flanking him. "What is it, honey?" he asked.

"My ankle," she groaned. "I'm fine—"

He gently lifted the hem of her pantleg, and cursed. "It's not fine."

His tone had her glancing down. Fuck. It wasn't fine. It was swollen already, and she could hardly feel her toes. "I'm going with Fred to the vet first," she said.

"No."

Two letters, one word, said so fiercely that she blinked.

"Claire will take Sweetheart, who's in my car, home. Baine will take Fred to your vet. Who you'll call right now, and if they're closed or can't take him, then he will take him to the emergency vet." She opened her mouth to protest. "Then as soon as these officers will allow us out of here, I'm taking you to the hospital."

"But—"

"Plus, Spence will be backup if either Claire or Baine need him," he said. "They have it, okay? Let me take care of you. Let me get you to the hospital."

The shorter officer with red hair nodded at her ankle. "Which should be right now." He passed Ben a card. "Call me when she's up to talking."

Ben nodded, shook his hand. "Thank you."

"Oh, my God!"

They all looked, saw Claire, her hair flowing behind her as she rushed into the room.

"Stef!" She dropped to her knees beside her. "Shit. Are you okay?"

Stef felt her eyes well. They hardly knew each other, and yet Claire was here, worry on her face, and her hand gripping Stef's tightly. "I'm fine," she said, but her voice broke, and a tear slipped out.

"Can you stay with Fred until Baine gets here?" Ben asked.

"Of course."

"I—"

Claire squeezed her hand, wincing and glancing down. Stef followed her gaze, saw that dark bruises were already appearing on her wrists. "Let us do this for you, okay? I'll text you updates for Fred every step of the way."

"But . . . why?"

"Because you're Ben's." A gentle smile. "And you're you."

CHAPTER THIRTY

Ben

CLAIRE WAS true to her word.

After Stef had called her vet, she and Baine, who'd arrived by then, got Fred to the vet, Sweetheart tagging along in her carrier.

Luckily for Fred, nothing was broken, and he would recover from his sprained foot and bruised ribs in another week or so.

Stef hadn't been so lucky.

Jeremy had fractured one of the small bones in her foot, and because of her past injury, she'd needed surgery to reset it.

Stef had just made it back to her room, after the hour-long surgery and then two hours in the recovery suite, but she was still groggy and sleeping off the aftereffects of the anesthesia, though she had asked for a Fred update the moment she realized Ben was in the room.

He was able to give her one—a good one—showing her the picture Claire had sent of Sweetheart and Fred curled up on a bed in the living room of his place.

"Tomorrow, we'll go back to my place," he said, brushing

back her hair. "Stay there until I can get an alarm system installed at yours. Then we can go to yours—"

Her eyes had closed. Her mouth gone slack.

But just before she'd drifted off again, she'd reached for his hand, lacing their fingers together, and he kept his vigil, his grip tight, as she slept through the night.

———

THE DETECTIVES LEFT on the same elevator that had brought Stef's gaggle of friends up.

Stef's face was drawn, but her eyes were happy.

Claire sat by her side, folded into the group whether because she was female or just had the right attitude or because that was the way they were, accepting whoever came into their periphery.

And they were all fussing, Heidi adjusting the pillow beneath Stef's ankle. Tammy bringing her a cup of hot chocolate, Kels searching through the guide for something that Stef would want to watch. Cora was making everyone laugh, and Kate had been gently brushing her hair, was now braiding the silken locks into a crown across her head.

"You look like shit," Baine said.

"I haven't had a chance to thank you," Ben said by way of answer.

Baine shook his head. "You know there's no thanks needed, not between us."

Ben *hadn't* known it, not really. He still wasn't used to reaching out for help. It had been easier to take care of everything for everyone else, rather than making himself vulnerable by asking for it.

But he wouldn't forget it now. Wouldn't *ever* forget it.

Red lips had shattered the wall around him, and he couldn't stop himself from caring . . . about Stef, about Baine and Claire, about Stef's friends. Because he'd watched her constantly finding herself unworthy of their affection, terrified they would take it away and leave her, and despite that, still finding the strength to give it, to care, to love.

He wasn't going to let that go.

"Thank you anyway," he said.

Baine rolled his eyes but nodded, turning for the elevator, just as cackling broke out in the living room, Claire no doubt telling more embarrassing stories about him. She and Baine had been staying at his place, managing the dogs and the business so that Ben could focus solely on Stef. Friends, not employees, and he was ashamed to think that it had taken him so long to realize that fact.

More cackling.

Baine winced as he stepped onto the elevator. "I'm going to rescue my ears from the noise." A smirk. "Good luck with yours."

"Fucker." But it was said without heat, his gaze on Stef, on the fading bruises on her wrists, the foot propped on the pillow, guilt eating at him.

Baine caught the elevator door, holding it open. "Hey," he said, eyes concerned. "You okay?"

He was a long shot away from okay—the sight of Stef pinned against the wall, her fucking ex with his hands on her, had brought back the nightmares he'd thought long gone. He'd hardly slept, dreaming of his father being dragged out of the car, blood soaking the street, of his mother taking her final rattling breath, of what might have happened to Stef if he'd been delayed, if he hadn't left work early because he was so anxious to see her.

Broken and bleeding, a final rattling breath.

He shuddered. Not okay.

Definitely not okay.

But he'd eventually be, if only for the woman who held his heart in her palm. Effortlessly caught and grasped tight, and he didn't give a shit that he'd been snared.

"No," he said, when Baine made to step off the elevator, despite the cackling rising in volume behind them. "I'm not okay," he admitted. "But I'll get there."

Baine studied him closely, his hand still on the elevator door.

"Ben? Are you all right?" Stef's soft voice trailed through the air, and Ben watched Baine's face gentle, even as he was already turning to face her.

A clap on his shoulder had him glancing back.

Baine nodded, stepped back and released him. "Yes," he said. "You will."

———

IT WAS MUCH LATER that the apartment was empty of everyone save the dogs, Fred curled up next to the couch, Sweetheart on Stef's lap, her fingers running through the soft, white fur.

Still, he couldn't imagine how the fuck she'd tamed the beast that Sweetheart had been—except that she'd tamed him, too . . . or perhaps, she'd soothed him.

Just like she'd soothed the jagged edges of Sweetheart missing his mom.

He sat on one end of the couch, Stef's head on his thigh.

And just as she ran her fingers through Sweetheart's fur, he stroked lightly through the locks of her hair, slowly undoing the braid she'd said was hurting her scalp.

"Is your ankle bothering you? Do you need your pain medicine?" he asked once it was out and the tangles were loosened, his voice soft, not wanting to break her relaxed state.

"No," she murmured.

He went back to stroking, memorizing the lines of her face, and for long minutes, neither of them spoke.

"I was going to cook for you," she whispered, and he blinked, pulling himself from the very quiet place he'd drifted into, calmed by her presence, thankful and happy to just be here, that she was safe and happy.

"What were you going to cook?" he asked.

"The one thing I can make that isn't breakfast. It's nothing fancy, a chicken and rice soup with vegetables. I'd just . . ." She swallowed. "I'd just needed to put the rice in it when I got there and . . ."

Quiet again.

He continued moving his fingers through her hair, not changing the rhythm, soothing her until she found her words again.

"Anyway, I'd wanted to cook for you because I'd finally realized you weren't like them—no, I'd always known you weren't like them. I was just too scared to let you in because . . ."

He'd gone stiff, fingers stilling, but forced himself to relax, to breathe, to resume his stroking.

"Because no one around me has ever really cared about me. Not my parents. Not my brother. Not anyone I dated." Her tongue darted out, danced across her bottom lip. "Not until I met Heidi, and she introduced me to the girls and . . . even then, I didn't believe it."

He inhaled.

She sat up carefully, putting Sweetheart on the floor. The dog grumbled at being displaced but curled up next to Fred and closed her eyes. Stef's face was soft as she shifted and studied Ben's face. "And then you came into my life, rather auspiciously." She smiled and touched his cheek, so gently, her brown eyes blazing with love. For *him*. "You showed me what it was like to have someone care for me. Showed and *showed* me until I actually started to believe it. Until it propelled me to look into myself and realize that I *was* worth someone's love."

"Stef," he whispered, his heart breaking for her, breaking and reforming. For her.

"You didn't press me to tell you why I held back," she said.

"You just showed me that you'd take me as I was, that every day you would be there when you promised you would." Her voice dropped until it was barely audible. "And I've never had that. Or at least, not that I could remember."

She winced, trying to turn to face him, so he carefully tucked a pillow behind her back and shifted around, moving to the other end of the couch, easing next to her propped-up foot and sitting so he could see her more easily.

"You told me a story once," she said. "So, I'm going to tell you one now."

He nodded.

"My brother was born just a year after me." Her throat worked. "Chance and I were Irish twins, but in reality, we were more like real twins. Babies at the same time, and once we were both walking and running, we hit most of those kid milestones at the same time—learning to read, playing catch, silly things like singing songs and dancing. He was ahead, I was behind. Always. He rode his bike first, tackled the scary obstacles at the park, the mean kids at school. He was . . . larger than life, and really, *really* good at everything. It was easy to get lost in his shadow, easy to disappear." Her eyes met his and drifted away. "My parents didn't notice when I scored a goal in soccer because he scored three, or scraped my knee learning to ride my bike because he was launching himself down steps or curbs or finding some new obstacle to tackle."

Ben reached over and grasped her hand, ran his finger over the back of it.

"And I probably should have been jealous of him, but Chance was . . . wonderful and I loved him. He had this spirit that surrounded him, a cloud that attracted people to him like flies. He was confident, bordering on cocky, but he was also kind. He didn't pick on people, even if they were . . . pale shadows of him."

Ben squeezed.

"Then he got sick," she whispered. "Or maybe he was

always on the edge of that. He lived a big life, but he also lived big downs. *Always*. And when we were ten—well, he was ten and I was almost eleven—things turned darker. Those lows grew until there were hardly any highs, until he couldn't get out of bed, until he'd lost joy in everything. Wouldn't go to school, wouldn't *live*. And my parents started bringing him to doctors, rightfully so. Therapists and medical doctors, so many specialists that it almost became an obsession."

She stared at the TV, blank as it was. "There wasn't a day he didn't spend with the doctors, or that my parents weren't researching, or on the phone searching for a way to make him better. Therapy didn't help, not for long anyway. He'd dive again, and they'd start over, but they couldn't get the medication right. He'd seem fine for a few days and then suffer."

A deep breath released slowly. "For ten years we lived and breathed that, everything on hold, all of us just barely existed. I didn't do anything but go to school and come home, and even at school, I existed as a buffer between Chance and anything that might knock him off track. If he couldn't go one day, I didn't go. If he needed to leave and go home, I brought him home or drove him when I was old enough."

A tear trailed down her cheek, and he longed to wipe it away, to take her in his arms, but he didn't want to stop her from telling her story.

So, he just clung to her hand and offered the only thing he could.

He listened.

"But eventually, I just couldn't do it anymore. I'd already delayed going to college, had stayed and gone to the community one in our hometown because I couldn't leave him, not when leaving might unbalance him, not when I wouldn't be there to protect him." She shook her head. "Then I couldn't breathe, found myself not wanting to. Instead, I was willing to let myself slip down and not exist and . . . that finally snapped me out of it."

"You left."

She nodded. "I had to."

He squeezed her hand again. "Yes, you did."

"I went off. I had two great months. It was amazing living in the dorms, surrounded by people who didn't want anything of me. And then . . ." Ben's throat seized, but he didn't press, just held her hand as she gathered her strength. "He killed himself."

His breath hissed out of him. "Oh, baby," he whispered. "I'm so sorry."

"My parents . . . they didn't explicitly blame me, but I saw the accusations in their eyes, in their sharp words when I returned for the funeral. Why hadn't I been able to give everything when they could?" Her eyes were unfocused, drawn back to that time. "I couldn't stand it, so the moment he was in the ground, I went back to school. Stayed there. Got my first boyfriend, lost my virginity, lost myself in trying to make people love me as much as my parents had loved Chance. But . . . college boys are, as you might remember, not inclined to love truly. They want to party and be free but . . . at the time, it seemed like further proof that I was unlovable, unworthy."

He couldn't stand this, but he had to, not only because she'd endured it, but because she needed him to shoulder this burden, to aid her in letting it go. Slowly, he tugged his hand free, leaned in carefully to cup her cheek, to brush the tears that continued to fall.

"Then I met Jeremy, and he was wonderful. At first. Or I thought he was, anyway, until I met you." She gave him a ghost of the smile. "I get now that our relationship was unbalanced. I gave. He didn't. Not in graduate school, when we met. Not after I moved here, and we were supposed to be building our future." Her hand covered his on her cheek. "I don't know why he broke up with me, why he pushed me away. Maybe part of him sensed that I was too desperate for him, too willing to do anything, he knew it would destroy me, so he turned me loose—"

Ben snorted.

She smiled sadly again. "You're probably right. I doubt it was anything altruistic. But he broke up with me brutally enough that I knew I wouldn't ever go back to him. Even though I was still desperate to feel loved, I couldn't forgive what he did and said and how he left me alone in a new state without a place to live and a broken heart."

"I want to kill him."

A chuckle slid from her lips. "After today, I don't think I would have minded. Especially after what he did to Fred." She shook her head, and he shook his. This woman and her dog, worrying over him rather than herself. "But it's better that he's gone, out of our lives forever."

"Our," Ben said, shifting closer to brush a kiss to her forehead. "I have to admit I like the sound of that."

Her lips turned up. "I do, too."

"Almost as much as I like the sound of *forever*."

Laughter on the air. "I like that, too." She covered his hand with her own. "You gave me that. Gave me a reason to hope, the strength to throw open the door and realize that I deserve more, not the crumbs that someone is inclined to toss my way. I deserve *everything*."

"Baby," he whispered.

"You, Ben," she added softly. "*You* gave that to me."

"I love you." His fingers slid over her cheek, into her hair. She sniffed, and he felt near enough to tears himself to ask lightly, "Do you think I could kiss you, if I'm very gentle?"

More laughter, this time in his ear, her smile beatific. "I really wish you would."

So he did.

CHAPTER THIRTY-ONE

Stef

It was Tammy's turn.

To keep her busy, or really, to keep her from going insane from being locked up in Ben's apartment.

Three weeks since Jeremy had broken into her place.

And somehow, she'd been coaxed into moving in with Ben.

Her condo was on the market, her things packed and moved to his place. The only thing that was missing was a back yard for Fred, not that her condo's had been anything to celebrate. A tiny postage stamp had nothing on it. Plus, Ben had already had grass installed on one of the patios for Sweetheart, and he'd had some workers expand it, so the pups would have more space to run.

It had worked out perfectly, and she was done with being scared and living in the past. She'd told him the dark secrets in her heart, the things that made her ashamed, that had her parents looking at her with disdain.

And he hadn't run.

He stayed.

He'd remained the Ben she knew and loved, and . . .

In the meantime, she convalesced, worked as much as she was able to from home, and Ben still had his hard stop at six, though oftentimes he was home much earlier, working beside her on the couch.

Yesterday, he'd brought home the news that Jeremy had pleaded guilty to his charges and would face both jail time and mandatory rehab.

Because what he'd been looking for that day when he'd broken in was oxycontin, leftover from her first surgery. She didn't know whether that was what he'd been looking for the first time he'd come earlier in the year, but she suspected it, suspected that the vase had just been an excuse to get into her house, one she'd unwittingly thwarted.

Temporarily, at least.

Because then he'd come back . . . and ruined her dinner plans.

She snorted, felt Tammy glance over at her. "What is it?" her friend asked, glancing up from her book.

She'd been reading while Stef watched, as she called it, another "boring pointy-ear show." But there was little to do besides read and watch TV, especially when she wasn't allowed to bear any weight on her ankle.

Tomorrow, though, she'd go back to the doctor, and if all looked good, then she'd be in a walking boot.

Woo-hoo.

The world would open up again.

"I'm just antsy," Stef said. "I need to get off my ass and *do* something."

Tammy laughed. "When's that supposed to happen?"

"Tomorrow. If I don't fuck it up."

"What could fuck it up?"

Stef rolled her eyes. "Nothing, according to Ben, so long as I keep my ass on this couch." She groaned. "Give me something. Distract me."

"How?" Tammy asked. "I'm boring and single and have absolutely no life outside of work."

"Tell me about work."

"You cannot possibly want to hear about that."

Okay, so maybe she didn't. "Tell me about your love life."

"I just told you I was single."

Stef groaned again. "Give me *something*. You're beautiful. Isn't there a guy or girl you're interested in?"

Tammy's voice was pained. "Now you sound like my mother. When are you going to get married, Tammy? You're the only one left, and you shouldn't work all the time. A man or a woman would settle you and—"

She broke off on a fake gag.

"No dating?" Stef asked.

"I'm not interested in turning into one of those sappy, love-struck idiots"—a grin—"no offense."

Stef *was* sappy, love-struck. The idiot part was questionable, she supposed, but she didn't take offense. Not when she supposed that everyone was a bit of an idiot when they were in love, especially when they were in love with a man like Ben.

"Ugh."

Stef blinked. "What?"

Tammy waved a hand. "*That.* You've got Ben-fog going on, dreaming about the man who holds your heart and all the rest of that barf-worthy nonsense." She slanted a look in Stef's direction, contrition in her gaze. "Not that I begrudge you your happiness. It's just . . ." Her lips pressed flat as she trailed off.

"You don't want that."

"No," Tammy agreed. "I don't. I just want to build my career and find success and . . . I guess, I just want to be me before I become an us." She sighed. "I don't know why everyone thinks that's so unreasonable."

She reached out and squeezed Tammy's hand. The other woman was a few years younger, just in her mid-twenties, as opposed to Stef's thirty-five. She had time to find herself. "I don't think it's unreasonable," she said. "Not at all." Another squeeze. "I think it's admirable. You have plenty of time to find someone, or not. And either way, you have time to make that decision."

Tammy smiled. "For a love-struck sap, you're not too bad."

Stef laughed. "Thanks for the vote of confidence."

A buzz had Tammy glancing down at her phone. "Oh, shoot that's the office. I need to take this."

"Go on," Stef told her. "And why don't you take off? Free yourself from my pointy-eared torture. Ben should be home soon, and I wouldn't want to subject you to more sappy lovey-dovey torture either."

Dancing brown eyes. "You sure?"

Stef nodded.

Tammy grinned, gathered up her book and her purse, said a quick goodbye, then answered the call as she disappeared into the elevator.

Stef was grinning as she turned her attention back to her show.

———

A CRASH WOKE her up with a start.

She blinked, saw the penthouse was dark, the sun having gone down beyond the windows.

Clearly, she'd fallen asleep. Had Ben come home and let her rest?

Her lips turned up at the corners, of course he had. He'd been nagging her about getting enough sleep so her body could heal properly. She didn't doubt he would have tiptoed by and taken care of the dogs and dinner.

Pushing her elbows beneath her, she sat up and glanced around.

Then nearly fell off the couch.

Ben was standing in the entryway, face hidden in the shadows, a bag at his feet, but there was something about the way he stood that had fear shivering down her spine.

"Why?" he asked, voice chilled as it slid along the air to her ears.

"Why what?"

He strode over, and she saw that his expression was furious and cold and completely unrecognizable.

This wasn't *her* Ben.

She knew that in an instant.

"I could have forgiven the movie being leaked. Thought it was just a mistake, that you loaned it to someone you shouldn't have." His jaw clenched as he crouched in front of her. "But then it was the details about the contract with Talbot Green, the confidential information of my deal to stream to Europe, the specifics about the new algorithm."

His fist banged down on the table.

"Was it worth it?" he asked. "What they paid you? Was it worth hurting me?"

"Ben," she breathed, swinging her leg down and sitting up fully. "I don't know what you think, but I didn't do anything—"

"You used my laptop," he interrupted. "When you came home from the hospital but hadn't gotten one from work yet. You went into my email and shared—"

This was madness.

"I didn't share or steal anything," she said. "This is all some stupid misunderstanding and—"

His voice was deadly soft. "Why did you do it?"

She pushed off the couch, squatted before him, ankle protesting the movement. She ignored the pain, both striking through her heart and shooting through the joint. "I didn't do anything. I promise you. I would never—"

"Except, you *did*."

She grasped his cheeks. "I *didn't*."

"Four isn't a coincidence, Stef," he said, not moving, his deep brown eyes boring into hers. "And you were the *only* one with the movie. The *only* one with access to my email and the other details. I didn't want to believe it—"

"Then don't," she begged. "Because. I. Didn't. Do. It."

Ben went still beneath her. Just stopped breathing, every muscle in his body going rock-hard. But there wasn't any heat in him, in his eyes.

No.

It was ice—pure and simple and biting, almost burning her with the intensity of the frost.

He jerked himself out of her grip.

"Get up."

Stef blinked. "What?"

"*Get up.*"

This time she didn't get a chance to even blink. Ben grasped her arm, yanked her up to her feet, and not all that gently either. Not like the tender, lovely man she'd grown to love.

The man who stood in front of her was a stranger.

He strode to where the bag sat, sitting on that white rug. "Get. Out."

"Ben," she began, wanting to beg, wanting to get him to see reason.

"I'll have your stuff sent back to your place, the realtor take your condo off the market."

Something cracked wide open in her chest. Her trust, her love, that all drifted away like clouds floating across the sky.

She tried one last time.

Because he was Ben. He'd shown that he was different. She wouldn't cower. She would fight for what they'd built, fight to hold on to all that was special between them.

"Don't do this," she whispered.

He bent, grabbed the bag, and strode to the elevator, waiting until the doors opened before he launched it onto the car. "Go," he snapped. "And feel privileged that I won't be suing you." He made a sound of disgust. "I can't believe that I ever thought you were different from *her*. From all those people who just wanted to get close to me, just wanted a piece of me. But you're not, are you? You're just like her. Probably laughing at my idiocy."

"I've never thought you were an idiot," she said. "I love you, so fucking much."

He scoffed.

And lips parting, a shaking sigh emerging, she stifled any further thoughts of begging, of trying to understand, trying to get him to believe her.

Because *fuck him.*

Because he'd given her the strength to do it, but she was the one who'd actually looked into herself and found worth and value, found a woman who could be loved.

Who *deserved* to be loved.

"Get the fuck out," he said in that icy tone of his.

"I'm gone," she said, limping toward the elevator, stopping only to grab her purse off that table in the entry, to pick up Fred's leash and snap it to his collar. He was excited for a moment, probably thinking it was walk time despite the dark skies outside. But when she didn't bring Sweetheart along, when she merely stroked that soft, white head and whispered, "Be good, Sweetie Pie," he slowed, glancing over his shoulder and giving a quiet whine.

Stef felt a sharp crack in her heart, pain radiating through her, but she pushed it down.

"Stay, Sweetheart," she said firmly when the dog started to rise.

Sweetheart plunked back down onto the fluffy bed.

Fred whined again.

That pain pulsed.

But she straightened and made her way to the elevator, proud her voice was completely neutral when she spoke. "I can't believe that I ever thought you were different," she said, anger drifting in, taking the place of all that hurt. She stopped in front of him, as he still held the elevator doors, despite the warning buzzer inside the cart, telling him to close them. His eyes were chips of ice, but she felt frosted over herself, and merely lifted her chin as she added, "I gave you pieces of myself that I've never given anyone. I *trusted* you. I—"

She broke off, shook her head.

"I loved you," she said and released a long, slow breath.

Then she pushed back his hand, tugged Fred forward, and they both stepped onto the elevator.

Ben stood there. No. Not Ben. Some stranger who she realized she didn't know at all.

The doors began to slide closed.

"And if you thought for one second, I could share with you what I shared," she said, stretching a hand out and stopping them once more. "If you thought I could conquer the demons I held tightly for so long to be with you, then could have turned around and sold your company's secrets for a quick buck, then you never knew me at all."

She let go.

The metal panels shut with a soft *snick*.

The elevator descended.

And then she left.

The first thing she did when she and Fred got into the Lyft she called was delete his texts and messages, block Ben's number, and set about erasing everything of him from her phone. Until she could almost pretend he didn't exist.

The next thing she did was wipe her eyes.

Because she was not going to cry.

Not over a man. Not ever again.

CHAPTER THIRTY-TWO

Ben

HE WASN'T a man who drank himself into oblivion.

Or he hadn't been.

But he'd changed.

Or at least, Stef had changed him.

Guzzling directly from the bottle of whiskey, he shoved himself into the corner between the TV stand and the windows, staring out at the city lights and ignoring Sweetheart when she nosed his side, probably wondering where Fred was. Well, she'd have to get used to being without him. Fred wouldn't be back, and neither would his owner. Not now. Not *ever*. He'd trusted Stef, given her everything he had, opened his heart and home and—

You never knew me at all.

Her words had echoed in his ear for the last hours, along with her smell filling his nose, her belongings in his sight.

This dark corner was the only place he'd found peace. Where he couldn't see her, scent her, *remember* her.

Except, he had the feeling he would *always* remember her.

"Fuck," he whispered, taking another guzzle.

It would be dawn soon, and he wanted to be black out drunk, to not remember, to—

"What the fuck are you doing?"

His head snapped back, cracking against the TV stand, the bottle slipping from his grasp, pouring all over the floor.

But he couldn't be bothered to pick it up, couldn't be bothered to do much of anything except ignore Claire as she strode toward him, her footsteps loud on the tile floor.

"Did you bathe in that on purpose?"

He flipped her off but didn't otherwise answer.

"Where's Stef?" she asked.

He kept his gaze determinedly on the buildings in the distance.

"Where is Stef?" she repeated stubbornly.

Well, he could be just as stubborn. Doubly so, if necessary. He clenched his teeth together and stared unseeing through the glass.

"What did you do?" She kicked his foot, jarring him away from the window, causing him to jerk his gaze to his. "What the fuck did you do?" she snapped.

"What I had to." His voice was raspy, hardly distinguishable from a growl.

"What does that mean?"

"Stef sold me out." He picked up the bottle. "So, I told her to go. I won't sue her for damages. I can't stomach that, not when —" He lifted it, sucked down some dredges. "I just can't."

"You told her to go?" Claire asked icily. "I thought we'd all decided to wait and see what the investigation yielded."

He sniffed. "I knew how it would go." Maybe if he got a straw, he could get the last little bit. "Knew it was the same as before."

Claire was suddenly in his face, knocking the bottle to the side. "It is *nothing* like before."

Something in her tone had the fog clearing slightly.

"What are you talking about?"

She gripped his shoulders. "It wasn't Stef who sold you out. It was *Spence*. The audit team discovered that about two hours ago." She shook him. "We said that we weren't going to do anything until we knew. You fucking promised and—"

"It was Spence?"

Her nails dug into his shoulders. "Yes."

"Not Stef?"

The pain from her grip focused him. "No. Not Stef."

Fuck. *Fuck!*

It wasn't Stef, and he'd said . . . *oh fuck*, he'd sent her away. He'd told her to go, and hadn't been there like he'd promised, and—

He stumbled to his feet.

He needed to go find her, to apologize, to—

Claire shoved him down. "Do you know what I received the moment I was out of that meeting? The moment I finally had a chance to breathe after spending the last sixteen hours working my ass off for you, for our company?" She didn't wait for him to respond. "I got a message from Stef saying that she didn't steal from Hunt, and that she wanted me to know that, and that she would be sorry to lose my friendship, because even though she was just getting to know me, she liked me a lot."

She heaved him back against the wall. "So you, motherfucker, are not going anywhere. You are going to sit there, sober the fuck up, and figure out how to beg her for forgiveness." A short, sharp breath. "And then you are going to come with me to the office so that we can be there when the lawyers and HR confront Spence."

He reached up, gripped his hair. "I fucked up."

"Yes, you did."

Scrambling to the coffee table, he grabbed his phone off it, dialed Stef's number. It rang and rang and rang, but she didn't pick up. He called again. It did the same thing. And the same on a third time. "Shit. *Shit.*"

"Shut up," Claire snapped, snatching the phone from his

hand. "Just shut the fuck up, get in the shower, deal with this shit at work, and start thinking."

"About what?"

"Finding some way to make this up to Stef, even if she doesn't take your sorry ass back," she said. "Because she deserves peace and a fucking apology."

She slammed the phone down on the table and walked to the elevator.

"Eight. Fucking. O'clock."

She jabbed the button to call the metal car.

"Don't be late."

———

HE WAS sober but felt like hell, even more so by the time he'd made it out of the meeting, his lawyers and HR department doing the heavy lifting.

Spence had confessed.

He might face criminal charges.

He'd called and texted Stef dozens of times from the moment he'd realized the truth.

But she hadn't picked up, hadn't called back.

Not that he blamed her.

He'd been . . . awful, worse than those who had hurt her.

"Fuck," he breathed, shoving out of the building and striding across the parking lot. He didn't know what to do, how to get through to her. He just knew that he had to talk to her, to apologize, to try and make things right.

He drove to her place, parked in the driveway, and got out of his car . . . just as she was limping up to her front door.

In a walking boot.

Shit. He'd forgotten that she had the appointment today.

Hurrying out of the car, he moved up the path and got to her porch the same time that she did, taking the purse from her hands.

She didn't fight him, just let him unlock the door and hold it wide for her, as she moved inside. Didn't say a word when he followed her in, when he closed the wooden panel behind himself.

Didn't say a word as Fred bounded over, just scratched his head and disappeared down the hall, the bedroom door clicking closed behind her.

He didn't know what to do, didn't know how to make this right.

So he waited in the hall, silently standing there and feeling like an intruder, and maybe he was.

The door opened, Stef now in pajamas, and she slowed, as though surprised he was still there. But she still didn't speak, only hesitated for a moment then moved into the kitchen.

"How did you get to your appointment?"

It was her right foot that was broken.

"A Lyft."

Fuck.

She turned away.

"It was Spence," he said.

A flash of brown eyes before she looked away. "I'm sorry," she murmured but didn't say anything further as she reached into the fridge and pulled out a carton of milk, grabbing a bar of chocolate and a cup from a bag on the counter. She had gone out and bought groceries, a mug, because her belongings were at his house.

And she was apologizing.

He moved, trapping her between his body and the counter. She didn't react, just broke off pieces of chocolate and placed them one by one into the mug. "I'm the one who should be saying sorry," he told her. "I—I didn't tell you all of my story before. I was engaged right when the company was taking off. She stole from me, from us, and . . ."

"I see."

She poured milk into the mug, pushed against his arm, and placed the cup into the microwave.

Still with her back to him, still hardly acknowledging his presence.

"I assumed wrong, and I treated you . . ." He blew out a breath, stared down at his feet, wondering how he could make this right. "*I* was wrong."

"I forgive you."

Surprise had his eyes flying up. "You forgive me?"

"I do."

But there was something off with her voice, with her expression.

"I forgive, but I want you to leave. To not come back. To—"

"Stef, no."

Her throat worked. "I can't hate you because you showed me what I deserve from a relationship, and I forgive you because we all make mistakes. But I can't have you in my life. You need to go."

"Stef," he said, getting onto his knees, grasping onto her thighs. "I'm literally begging you to give me another chance. To let me be the man you deserve."

Silence as she studied his face closely.

"No."

His heart sank.

"Leave, Ben. And don't come back."

He didn't know what to say. He didn't know how to make this right, couldn't treat this like a business deal that had gone this wrong, couldn't salvage something this fucked, and he certainly didn't have the words to ensure she gave him another chance.

So, he did the only thing he could.

He walked out the front door and left Stef to her life.

CHAPTER THIRTY-THREE

Stef

THE LETTER ARRIVED the next morning, left on her front porch.

But she didn't open it.

Just set it on the counter, met her Lyft out front, and went to work, her first day back in weeks.

Heidi took one look at her and opened her mouth, but Stef merely lifted a hand and begged to give her an explanation another time. Preferably never, but she knew she wouldn't be so lucky, so she just had to hope that it would hurt a little less by the time she was interrogated by her friend.

Then she'd worked.

Straight through breaks and lunch and all the way until it was time to leave. Heidi had only spoken to her about non-work stuff once, asking softly, "Are you okay?"

To which she'd answered, "No, but I will be."

And when she got back home that evening, saw the letter on the counter, she read it . . . and it didn't change anything. He'd explained more in depth about his former fiancée, who betrayed him and hurt his business right when it was just getting under-way, but . . . it didn't make one fucking bit of difference.

Not when he'd thought she was capable of that.

Not when she'd thought he was different, and he'd broken that trust.

Not when . . . she had loved him and—

So she forgave him because she understood how the past might hurt someone, might make it so damned difficult to live in the present . . . but she'd given him every part of her, and he'd thrown it back into her face.

She wasn't a punching bag. She deserved respect.

One apology and a letter didn't erase that.

———

FLOWERS ARRIVED THE NEXT DAY. Sunflowers, in fact, which were her favorite, of course. She'd expect nothing else of Ben, the sweet Ben, trying to win her over.

She wanted to throw them in the trash.

Because when would he become angry Ben again?

Despite that, the cheerful yellow blooms stayed on her counter, and every time she looked at them, her heart melted a little bit.

She hadn't told him her favorite, but he'd found out.

Stupid? Yes.

But just because she kept the flowers didn't mean she was going to let Ben back into her life.

———

THERE WAS a car in her driveway.

She wanted to ignore it, but the driver exited it the moment she stood on the porch, pausing to lock her door.

"Ms. McKay?"

Stef glanced up.

"I'm to drive you to work."

She sighed, thought about arguing, but instead just canceled the Lyft she'd ordered, allowed the driver to assist her into the car, and accepted the ride.

She didn't want to be late.

———

CHOCOLATES AND A FRIDGE full of groceries.

A new leash and collar for Fred.

A *Stargate* script signed by the whole cast.

The car at her disposal, every single day.

And more flowers, so many sunflowers that her condo threatened to explode with them.

But not her promised belongings.

She only had the bag he'd packed, the minimal clothes, and when she had unblocked his number to ask him for the rest of her things, he'd said she was welcome to get them herself.

She was welcome to go to his place and pack them up.

Seriously?

The balls on the man.

She hadn't responded.

But he had.

I love you.

He'd sent that multiple times per day.

Along with,

I'm sorry. Please give me another chance.

And both were punctuated with pictures of Sweetheart.

She should have blocked his number again, but those pictures had her hesitating, and she didn't reply to any of the messages, nor pick up the phone calls he made morning and night.

Though she listened to the voicemails he left.

Over and over again.

Sick. She was absolutely sick.

But she didn't block him.

Or throw out the sunflowers, the script. She ate the chocolates, used the leash, and when she came home from work to find the box on her porch, she nearly began crying.

Because inside was a hoodie.

One of Ben's, the spiced scent in her nose, the worn material like velvet on her skin. She'd put it on, and hadn't taken it off, hadn't turned away the food he'd had delivered, nor the custom walking boot adorned with her name in pink glitter that arrived the next day.

"Fuck," she whispered, holding it close to her chest.

Fred had jumped on the couch and cuddled close, and she knew that it was the hoodie. He'd gone crazy looking for Ben the night before, when she'd come in with the sweatshirt.

She knew the feeling.

"Oh, Ben," she whispered, running her fingers over the boot. "What are you doing?"

What was *she* doing? She was miserable without him, missed spending time with him, sitting on the couch, watching TV, eating together, making love, and staying up all hours of the night talking.

But if she went back to him, accepted his groveling and apologies, what did that make her?

She'd fought to be strong, fought to finally find her worth, and if she accepted back a man who'd talked to her like that, who'd kicked her out of his place without cause, without talking it through with her, then how could she say she was whole, that she was valuable and worthwhile?

She couldn't.

She just . . . couldn't.

Sighing, she set the boot on the floor, curled up with Fred, and lost herself in the world of fantasy.

It was so much better than real life.

———

"ALL RIGHT," Heidi snapped, tossing down her notebook. "We're done for today. Everyone out."

They all froze and looked at each other, weighing her seriousness and judging it to be fierce. They'd had a shit day, experiments going wrong, data going missing.

Because of Stef.

Because she'd been up half the night trying to figure out if she could call Ben and thank him for the boot.

Stupid, huh?

Heidi cleared her throat, and she along with the interns, rose and move toward the door.

"Not you."

Stef glanced up, saw her boss's eyes fixed on hers.

Fuck.

The girls had come over a couple of days before, and she'd told them everything. They'd been suitably upset for her and absolutely furious at Ben. Including Claire, who'd surprised Stef by showing up at all, and who'd chimed in additional details as they'd all cursed all of Ben's bad character traits.

That had felt good—that they all were on her side.

But it had also felt bad.

Because she'd realized that for all the bad in that one moment in the penthouse, she'd missed their time together, missed . . .

Ben.

She missed him.

There. She admitted it.

Was that such a terrible thing?

She kind of thought it was.

"What are you doing?" Heidi asked, once everyone else had gone.

Stef blinked, glanced up. "What do you mean?"

"I mean, you're absolutely miserable, but you haven't even talked to him," Heidi snapped, tossing up her hands as she moved around the lab table. "I *mean*, you're in love with the man and he fucked up, but he's spent the better part of the last two weeks trying to make it up to you."

"That—"

"Doesn't mean what he did was right," Heidi said. "Of course, it doesn't. But you're miserable and he fucked up and he's apologized. I want to flay him open for hurting you, but, babe, he's *trying to make it right*."

Stef swallowed hard.

"He's going to mess up," Heidi said. "That's part of being a fucking human. But part of being a good person, a good man, is what he does in the wake of that."

Stef's heart pounded, her pulse shuddering through her veins. She closed her eyes, letting Heidi's words wash over her, remembering all the things Ben had done, both before and after that one horrific moment in the penthouse, remembering that moment, too.

And how she hadn't broken.

How she'd stood up for herself.

She could have done better, too, could have refused to leave, shouted and fought until he heard her.

She'd left.

But she also hadn't withered and made herself small.

Stef sank onto her stool as the realization struck home, echoing through every part of her—she wasn't going to be that person again, the girl used by everyone.

"No matter what," she whispered. "I won't be her again."

"No, you won't," Heidi said.

Her eyes met her friend's. "He messed up."

Heidi nodded. "He was an asshole," she agreed. "Just like we all are sometimes, but you didn't let him walk all over you."

"I didn't," Stef said. "And he's trying to make it right."

"Plus, he's doing it in glorious fashion," Heidi said, her voice lightening. "He apologized with style, held nothing back, and he's not giving up."

"He's a good man," she whispered, and knew it to be the truth.

"Yes."

"And now I have to decide what to do, because we can't go on like this forever."

A smile. "Also, yes."

Stef fell silent.

"For the record," Heidi said. "I think you should keep him."

CHAPTER THIRTY-FOUR

Ben

THE ELEVATOR DOORS opened on a ding, but he'd long ago stopped hoping it would be Stef.

He had so much to make up for.

So much to prove.

It might take forever for her to accept him back into her life.

And rightfully so.

He'd been . . . well, words couldn't describe how much of an asshole he'd been.

Pathetic. Angry. Stupid. Horrible. Oh, and he might as well throw undeserving in there as well.

Just for good measure.

He had the TV on in the background, the show a painful reminder, and yet he felt the need to keep punishing himself. Because it was part of her. Part of Stef. And he'd take any piece he could get.

"*Stargate?*"

He jumped, launching himself off the couch, dislodging a very unhappy Sweetheart.

Stef was here.

Here.

A kernel of hope gathered in his chest, he started to round the couch, wanting to take her in his arms, but she put her hand up, and he stopped in his tracks.

"I missed you," he said. "And I'm so sorry and I love you and I'll make it up—"

Her hand lifted higher.

He shut up.

"You will never, *ever* talk to me like that again."

That kernel grew, spreading outward from his chest. "I promise you, I won't."

"And you won't order me to leave or shut me down." Her shoulders rose and fell on a breath. "You will talk to me. We will work out our problems. Together."

"Yes, honey. I swear to you that we will be in this together."

"And you will also understand that it will take me time to trust you again."

That dimmed the kernel, but he knew it wasn't anything less than he deserved. "I understand. I . . ." He hesitated. "Can I show you something?"

She nodded.

He brought her the stack of paper he'd intended on having delivered in the morning, pressed them into her hands.

She flipped through them, her mouth gaping open.

"I—" Her eyes shot to his. "I . . . you're giving me a *building?*"

"I don't want you to ever think that you don't have a place here," he said, daring to brush his knuckles over her cheek. "So, it's yours. This floor, the rest of the building. It's all yours. You have the leverage, the right to kick *me* out if you want. You *belong* here."

A single tear slid down her cheek. "Ben," she whispered.

"I know you said you forgave me, but I haven't begun to forgive myself. I'm so sorry. You told me all your weak spots, you found courage to plaster them up and move forward, and I —I broke—"

His voice cracked, tears blurred his eyes.

Soft fingers on his cheek. "You didn't break me."

He sucked in a breath. "I'm—"

"No more apologies, baby. No more looking back." Her lips curved. "You were an asshole. But I should have fought to make you see—"

"I wouldn't have let you."

She stepped close enough that her breath brushed his lips. "Let's call it that we both fucked up—you significantly more than me, of course—" Her mouth curved. "And move on, okay?"

"I feel like I should be groveling more."

"You gave me a *building*." She held up the papers. "And a signed script and chocolate and sunflowers and a glittery boot with my name on it . . . and I'm never giving you that sweatshirt back, not for as long as you live."

"You can have every single one in my closet, all that I haven't bought yet. They're all yours."

"Such romantic words." A grin. "If only we weren't talking about hoodies."

"Would you rather me talk about you?"

Humor in her eyes. "Yes."

"Okay then, let's start with these beautiful, gorgeous brown eyes. I can stare at them for hours and still not discern all the secrets."

"Ben."

"And these lips." He ran his thumb along the bottom one. "I could taste them for days and—"

"*Ben.*"

"—and still never be satisfied." She moaned, but he kept going. "And this heart." He stroked his fingers along her chest, just over where it pounded against her rib cage. "It's huge and brave, and I am utterly amazed at its strength."

"Ben!"

"What?"

"Just shut up already and kiss me."

"I love you, and I just have to tell you one more thing."

"Ben," she groaned. "What is it?"

"I'm going to kiss you now."

She burst out laughing.

And when he finally got to slant his mouth across hers, her laughter slid across his tongue, filled his heart and soul to overflowing.

It was the best thing he'd ever tasted.

EPILOGUE

Stef, one year later

SHE SMILED when she woke up.

But she did that a lot now.

In fact, she did it every day, but most especially on mornings like this. Saturday sleep in days and beach days and work days and . . . his arm tightened around her waist, his lips pressing to her nape.

Every day.

She woke up happy every single day.

Because she had Ben.

And herself. That was just as important.

"Morning," Ben murmured, his voice husky as his hand slid down between her thighs. The man had skills like that, could easily arrow right to the spot that would bring her the most pleasure.

Not just in bed, either.

Her whole life was happier.

And not just because she lived in a penthouse, either. Though she couldn't lie that the view was good. Maybe even incredible, if one considered the naked man in bed next to her.

Okay, not maybe.

It *was* incredible.

Ben's fingers brushed over her clit, and she moaned, shifting her thighs apart so he could reach better—

Right as two furry bodies launched themselves onto their bed.

Ben groaned, not in pleasure this time.

But Stef just laughed. "They know it's beach day."

Ben groaned again, but it was good-natured this time. "I'm up," he groused as Fred climbed on top of him, licking his face. "I'm up."

Except he didn't get up.

Instead, he rolled to the side, retrieved something, and said to Fred, "Give this to your mom, would you?"

And like the good boy he was, Fred turned and deposited whatever it was onto her lap. It took her a minute to fish the drool-covered box out of the blankets, then another to push Fred and Sweetheart back enough for her to sit up.

"What's this?" she asked breathlessly.

Even though she already had a good idea of what it was.

Ben just smirked. "You'd find out if you opened it."

"Or you could tell me."

"Or"—he pressed her fingers to the lid—"you could just open it and find out."

"Or—"

"Stef." He leaned up, kissed her until her lungs threatened to explode. "Open the damned box."

She started to, stopped. "It better not be another building."

"*Stef.*"

She opened the box, gasped, even though she'd already known what was inside. Because the ring was beautiful and exquisite and too much and . . . she loved it. Loved *him*.

So freaking much.

"Will you—"

"Yes!"

She launched herself into his arms, kissing him with every bit of love and joy and affection she possessed for this man. But she only got to kiss him for a few heartbeats before two furry beasts joined in on the party.

Four tongues in the mix wasn't ideal.

But those other three tongues were also her family.

Which, she got, sounded gross and weird and wholly unappetizing.

Still, they were her family, even with the dual doggy breath, even with Sweetheart wriggling between them, licking her chin and Fred knocking the air out of her as he climbed on top of her to settle on her chest.

Even with Ben—

No, *especially* with Ben, smiling down at her as he dodged paws—and tongues—to slide the ring on her finger, proving to her day in and out that he was a good man.

The perfect man for her.

"I love you," she whispered.

"I—"

There was a clamoring in the hall, and they froze.

"Did you ask her yet?" Claire.

"Did she say yes?" Heidi.

"I brought breakfast!" Kate.

"I don't think we should be here." Kels.

"We should definitely be here, if only to get a shot at seeing Ben naked." Tammy.

A cackle. Cora. "I think you're my favorite friend."

The dogs jumped off the mattress and sprinted from the bedroom, as though finally realizing people who would love on them were just mere feet away.

"Sweet Christ," Ben muttered.

Stef tugged the covers up. "What are they doing here?"

Ben winced. "I might have accidentally mentioned that I was going to propose this morning."

She glared.

Another wince. "Does that yes still stand?"

God, she loved him. "Yes," she whispered, rolling so she was on top of him. "It's still a yes. Because my friends are punishment enough—"

"Hey!"

She darted a glance to the entrance to the bedroom, saw her friends crammed into the door. "I said, yes, now go," she ordered. "And shut the door behind you."

They went.

But not before Cora whined, "But we didn't get to see—"

They closed the door.

Stef was left alone with her man.

And *she* was the lucky one to see him naked.

EPILOGUE
BAD GIRLFRIEND

Tammy

Are you really breaking up with me via text?

TAMMY WINCED as she read the text message and started to set down her cell.

But it vibrated again.

While I'm in your bathroom?

Yeah, so her timing wasn't ideal.

Sighing, she tugged the covers back and pulled on her robe. Her frumpy, holey, old flannel robe that absolutely dwarfed her and was so unappealing that it had run off more than her fair share of men.

Which was why she only pulled it out for very special occasions.

Her period when she felt horrible and crampy and exhausted and just wanted to veg on the couch and pretend that her uterus wasn't shredding itself to pieces.

The other very special occasion?

This.

The bathroom door cracked open as she was belting it, and a very pretty, probably too pretty for her man walked out. Naked. She picked up his clothes, turned them right side out, and handed them to him.

"This is me breaking up with you. Not in the bathroom," she added when he opened his mouth to say something she didn't want him to say. "Not that we were together in the first place."

"We've been sleeping together for three months."

She lifted a brow. "We've been fucking together. That's it. That's what I made clear from the moment I brought you home from Bobby's."

"That's not—"

He broke off, and she pointed to the clothes. "Get dressed," she ordered, moving to the bedroom door. "I'll clue you in. You're upset because you're usually the one who ends things, and you're used to women fawning all over you because you're pretty." A beat. "And you are. You're gorgeous."

His face went soft, and Tammy remembered why she'd brought him home in the first place.

But the man was getting too attached.

It would be much less messy to end things now.

"But I'm done."

"But—"

"Done," she repeated, having done this too many times to do anything but end it here and now. Adam was a nice guy, and she'd kept him around for so long because he'd seemed on board to be a fuck buddy, but tonight . . . tonight he'd been different.

Tonight he'd made love to her.

Tonight hadn't been about mutual attraction.

He had feelings for her, and she couldn't let that stand. Better to cut ties now before he grew even more attached, before things got messier.

"Get dressed," she said again, exiting the bedroom and walking down the hall, moving to the front door.

It was better to be by an exit.

That made things less complicated . . . and easier to slam and lock the door.

A minute later, Adam emerged from the bedroom, shoving his cell and wallet into his pocket, his eyes blazing, his lips parting as he lifted his arms, preparing to take her in his arms.

Fuck.

She sidestepped, gripped the doorknob, and opened the door.

"Bye, Adam," she murmured.

"We'd be good together."

"No," she said. "We wouldn't."

"You like me."

She clenched her jaw. "Look, you're a nice guy, but—"

He came close, lowered his head.

She put up her hand, pushed him back. "No."

"Tammy—"

"It's not you. It's me."

That finally seemed to penetrate, probably since it was such a shitty line, a crappy thing to say. But Adam at least backed away, his eyes furious. "Seriously?"

Tammy just lifted her brows.

He made a disgusted sound, but she was far too well-versed in this to feel guilty.

"Goodbye, Adam."

A shake of his head, but he didn't say anything further, just walked down the steps.

She watched him get into his car, screech out of her driveway.

Sigh.

Now she'd need to find a new source of orgasms.

Rolling her shoulders, she started to turn to go back inside.

"It's not you, it's me?"

That voice was silk brushing along her thighs, dipping up to test the moisture between them. It was heat in her abdomen, fingers grazing her nipples.

It was . . . instant sexual attraction, the same heady feeling she'd experienced the moment she'd laid eyes on Fletcher King. Eyes catching as she'd strode to her office, blazing blue irises and dark brown hair, so dark that it was nearly black. She'd clocked sexy stubble, a built body, and a great smile.

But he wanted *it.*

It being a real relationship, a girlfriend, a wife and the picket fence. *It* being everything she couldn't give, because she wasn't a relationship, girlfriend, or wife and picket fence kind of woman.

She wanted free . . . and freedom.

More than she wanted the gorgeous man in front of her.

"What are you doing here, Fletcher?"

"I need a favor."

The refusal was already on her lips. A favor that brought her sexy co-worker to her house on a weekend certainly didn't bode well for her.

But then he smiled, and she actually had to force her knees to lock so she didn't melt into a puddle and . . . *that* right there illustrated just how much she didn't want to be in a relationship.

Because she'd been resisting this attraction with Fletch for an entire year.

Locking her knees, ignoring the melting, denying the temptation of him.

But that sexy smile, highlighted by the setting sun, the warm lights of her porch . . . undid her.

That sexy smile had her refusal staying lodged in her throat.

That smile had her saying . . . *yes.*

—BAD GIRLFRIEND SEPTEMBER 14TH, 2021

BAD GIRLFRIEND

Tammy and Fletcher's story is coming September 14, 2021.
Preorder your copy at www.books2read.com/BadGirlfriend

———

Hate missing Elise's new releases? Love contests, exclusive excerpts and giveaways?

Then signup for Elise's newsletter here!

http://eepurl.com/bdnmEj

———

BILLIONAIRE'S CLUB

Bad Night Stand

Bad Breakup

Bad Husband

Bad Hookup

Bad Divorce

Bad Fiancé

Bad Boyfriend

Bad Blind Date

Bad Wedding

Bad Engagement

Bad Bridesmaid

Bad Swipe

Bad Girlfriend

ALSO BY ELISE FABER

Caged

Crashed (July 27th, 2021)

Cycled (October 5th, 2021)

Breakers Hockey **(all stand alone)**

Broken

Boldly (August 31st, 2021)

KTS Series

Fire and Ice (Hurt Anthology, stand alone)

Riding The Edge

Crossing The Line

Leveling The Field

Love, Action, Camera (all stand alone)

Dotted Line

Action Shot

Close-Up

End Scene

Meet Cute

Love After Midnight **(all stand alone)**

Rum And Notes

Virgin Daiquiri

On The Rocks

Sex On The Seats

Life Sucks Series **(all stand alone)**

Train Wreck

Hot Mess

Dumpster Fire

Clusterf*@k (August 16th, 2021)

Roosevelt Ranch Series **(all stand alone, series complete)**

Disaster at Roosevelt Ranch

Heartbreak at Roosevelt Ranch

Collision at Roosevelt Ranch

Regret at Roosevelt Ranch

Desire at Roosevelt Ranch

Phoenix Series **(read in order)**

Phoenix Rising

Dark Phoenix

Phoenix Freed

Phoenix: LexTal Chronicles **(rereleasing soon, stand alone, Phoenix world)**

From Ashes

In Flames

To Smoke (October 18th, 2021)

Stand Alones

Someday, Maybe (YA)

ABOUT THE AUTHOR

USA Today bestselling author, Elise Faber, loves chocolate, Star Wars, Harry Potter, and hockey (the order depending on the day and how well her team -- the Sharks! -- are playing). She and her husband also play as much hockey as they can squeeze into their schedules, so much so that their typical date night is spent on the ice. Elise changes her hair color more often than some people change their socks, loves sparkly things, and is the mom to two exuberant boys. She lives in Northern California. Connect with her in her Facebook group, the Fabinators or find more information about her books at www.elisefaber.com.

f facebook.com/elisefaberauthor

a amazon.com/author/elisefaber

BB bookbub.com/profile/elise-faber

O instagram.com/elisefaber

g goodreads.com/elisefaber

P pinterest.com/elisefaberwrite